"I've booked us a room," Adam announced calmly

"You've done what?" Leonie gasped. "You can't be serious. Only married people sneak off to hotels for the afternoon!"

"We are married."

"I mean people who aren't married to each other." She glared at him in frustration.

"But isn't this more exciting?" he teased.

It was exciting, there was no denying that. Leonie could feel the heat in her veins at the thought of spending the afternoon with Adam. But they couldn't. "Adam, I have to get back to work, and so do you," she protested.

Adam shook his head. "I told you, I intend concentrating on my reluctant lover. I cancelled all my appointments for this afternoon so that I could spend the time with you," he told her huskily. "I also told your boss I would need you all day."

Books by Carole Mortimer

These books may be available at your local bookseller.

Don't miss any of our special offers. Write to us at the following address for information on our newest releases.

Harlequin Reader Service
P.O. Box 52040, Phoenix, AZ   85072-2040
Canadian address: P.O. Box 2800, Postal Station A,
5170 Yonge St., Willowdale, Ont.   M2N 6J3

CAROLE MORTIMER

lovers in the afternoon

Harlequin Books

TORONTO • NEW YORK • LONDON
AMSTERDAM • PARIS • SYDNEY • HAMBURG
STOCKHOLM • ATHENS • TOKYO • MILAN

For
John, Matthew
and Joshua

Harlequin Presents first edition October 1985
ISBN 0-373-10829-X

Original hardcover edition published in 1985
by Mills & Boon Limited

CHAPTER ONE

WHAT was this man *doing* in her bed!

Dear God, it wasn't even her bed but his, she remembered now. She had been introduced to him at his office only that afternoon, and five hours later here she was in his bed!

She looked down at the man sleeping so peacefully at her side, one strong arm flung back across the pillow as he lay on his back, dark hair silvered with grey, all of his body deeply tanned, from a holiday he had taken in Acapulco he had told her over dinner. And she was well aware of the beauty of all that body, had touched every inch of it, from the broad shoulders, muscled chest with its covering of brown-grey hair, taut flat waist, powerfully built thighs, down long supple legs. The black silk sheet was pushed back to his waist now to reveal the strength of his chest and arms, the thick dark hair disappearing in a vee past his navel and down.

Her gaze returned quickly to his face. It was a strong, powerful face even in sleep, a wide intelligent forehead, widely defined eyebrows, beneath the long-lashed lids were eyes of a piercing grey, a long straight nose, firm uncompromising mouth, and a jaw that was firm as he slept. He was one of the most attractive men she had ever seen, or was ever likely to see, and she had spent most of the evening here in this bed with him, the first man to make love to her since her separation from her husband eight months ago.

7

But why did it have to be Adam Faulkner, rich industrialist, sixteen years her senior at thirty-nine, and her most recent client with the interior designing company she worked for!

She had gone to work so innocently this morning, had got out of bed at her usual seven-thirty, fed the fish and cat, warned the cat not to eat the fish while she was out all day, got her usual breakfast of dry toast and black coffee, both of which she consumed on her way to the shower as she usually did, applied the light make-up to her heart-shaped face and ever-sparkling green eyes, styled her feathered red-brown hair into its usual mass of uncontrolled lengths to her shoulders before donning the tailored blue suit and lighter blue blouse that made her hair look more red than brown, the white camisole beneath the blouse clearly the only covering to her unconfined breasts.

She had gone down to the underground car-park to her delapidated VW, sworn at it for the usual ten minutes before it deigned to start. She had then emerged out into the usual helter-skelter of traffic that was London in the rush-hour, dodging the other seasoned drivers as she drove to her office at Stevenson Interiors, cursing the fact that she needed to take the car at all, but the reliable London underground system went nowhere near her flat or the office. Yes, it had been a pretty usual day up to that point in time.

Her breathless entrance on to the sixth floor that housed the employees of Stevenson Interiors, after being stuck in the lift for fifteen minutes was also usual; the lift broke down at least once a week, and Leonie was usually in it when it did. It would have been *unusual* if she weren't!

'The lift again?' Betty, the young, attractive receptionist, asked ruefully.

'Yes,' her sigh was resigned. 'One of these days I'm going to fool it and take the stairs.'

'All twelve flights?' Betty's eyes widened.

Leonie grimaced, running controlling fingers through her flyaway hair. 'That would be a little drastic, wouldn't it?' she conceded wryly.

Betty handed her her messages. 'In your state of physical *un*fitness it could be suicide!'

'Thanks!' She skimmed through the pieces of paper she had been given, dismissing all of them as unimportant before pushing them into her navy blue clutch-bag. 'What's on the agenda for today?' she looked at Betty with her usual open expression.

'The staff meeting at nine o'clock?'

'Nine——! Oh Lord,' Leonie groaned, already fifteen minutes late for the meeting David had warned all employees *not* to be late for. 'Maybe if I just crept into the back of the room . . .?' she said hopefully.

'David would notice you if you crept in on your hands and knees and stood hidden for the whole meeting,' Betty told her derisively.

The other woman was right, of course. David had picked her out for his individual attention from the moment he had employed her six months ago, and although she occasionally agreed to have dinner with him she made sure it was only occasionally, not wanting any serious involvement, even if David was one of the nicest men she had ever known. An unsuccessful marriage had a way of souring you to the idea of another permanent relationship. Besides, David had little patience with the way things just seemed to happen to her, believing she should be able to have some control over the accidents that just seemed to occur whenever she was around.

She remembered another man, her husband, who had also found these accidents irritating, and she didn't need that criticism in her life a second time. She could handle these 'incidents' left to her own devices, she didn't need some man, no matter how nice he was, constantly criticising her.

'I'll creep in anyway.' She narrowly missed walking into the pot-plant that seemed to be following her about the room. 'What do you feed this on?' She looked up at the huge tree-like plant in horror. 'It's taking over reception, if not the world!'

'A little love and conversation do seem to have done the trick,' Betty acknowledged proudly. 'Now shouldn't you be getting to the staff meeting?'

David's office was crowded to capacity as she squeezed into the back of the room, but nevertheless his reproachful gaze spotted her instantly, although he didn't falter in his flow of how well the company was doing, of how good new contracts were coming their way every day.

Leonie yawned boredly, wishing she had been stuck in the lift even longer than she had been, receiving another censorious glare from David as she did, plastering a look of interest on to her face that she had perfected during her marriage, while her thoughts wandered to the Harrison lounge she had just completed, as pleased with the result as the elderly couple had been. She always felt a sense of immense satisfaction whenever she completed a job, knew she was good at what she did, that she was at last a success at something. Although some people would have her believe differently.

'Leonie, did you hear me?'

She looked up with a start at David's impatiently spoken question, blushing guiltily as she realised she was the cynosure of all eyes. 'Er——'

'Steady,' Gary warned as he stood at her side, deftly catching the papers she had knocked off the top of the filing cabinet as she jumped guiltily, grateful to the man who had taken her under his experienced wing from the day she came to work here.

Her blush deepened at the sympathetic ripple of laughter that filled the room; everyone knew of her habit of knocking and walking into things. 'Of course I heard you, David,' she answered awkwardly, her gaze guilelessly innocent as she looked at him steadily.

'Then you don't mind staying for a few minutes after the others have gone back to their offices?' he took pity on her, knowing very well that she hadn't been listening to a word he said.

'Er—no, of course not,' she replaced the papers on the filing cabinet that Gary had caught for her, wondering what she was guilty of now, feeling like the disobedient child that had been asked to stay in after school. It couldn't be her lack of attention to what was being said that was at fault, she never did that anyway, and David knew it.

She moved to sit on the edge of his desk as the others filed out to go back to work. 'Good meeting, David,' she complimented brightly.

'And how would you know one way or the other?' he sighed, looking up at her, a tall loose-limbed man with wild blond hair that refused to be tamed despite being kept cut close to his head, the rest of his appearance neat to precision point. He was only twenty-eight, had built his interior designing business up from a two-room, three-man operation to the point where he had a dozen people working for him. And Leonie knew she was lucky to be one of them, that Stevenson Interiors was one of the most successful businesses in its field, and that it was all due to David's drive and initiative.

She grimaced. 'Would it help if I were to say I'm sorry?' she cajoled.

'You always are,' David said without rancour. 'I wanted to talk to you about Thompson Electronics.'

A frown marred her creamy brow. 'Has something gone wrong? I thought they were pleased with the work I did for them. I don't understand——'

'Calm down, Leonie,' he ordered impatiently at her impassioned outburst. 'They were pleased, they *are* pleased, which is why the new President of the company wants you to personally design the decor for his own office suite.'

'He does?' she gasped.

'Don't look so surprised,' David mocked. 'It was a good piece of work. Even I would never have thought of using that particular shade of pink—indeed any shade of pink, in a group of offices.'

'It was the brown that off-set the femininity of it. You see I had——'

'You don't have to convince me of anything, Leonie,' he drawled. 'Or them either. You just have to get yourself over there at four o'clock this afternoon to discuss the details.'

She was still relatively new at her job, and tried to make every design she did a work of art, something personal; she was more than pleased to know that someone else had seen and appreciated some of her completed work enough to ask for her personally. It was the first time it had happened.

'Mrs Carlson will be expecting you,' David continued. 'She phoned and made the appointment first thing this morning. And she'll introduce you to the President then.'

'Ronald Reagan?'

He gave a patiently humouring sigh. 'Where do you get your sense of humour from?'

She grinned at him. 'It's what keeps my world going.'

David frowned at the underlying seriousness beneath her words. Except for the friendly, and often loony façade she presented to everyone here, he knew little about the real Leonie Grant. Her employee's file said she had been married but was now separated from her husband, but she never spoke of the marriage or the man she had been married to, her openness often seeming to hide a wealth of pain and disillusionment.

But it never showed, and Leonie found as much humour in her clumsiness as everyone else did, able to laugh at herself and the things that happened to her.

His mouth quirked into a smile. 'I have to admit that when Mrs Carlson said the President would expect you at four o'clock the same thought crossed my mind!'

'Naughty, David,' she shook her head reprovingly, her eyes glowing deeply green.

For a moment they shared a smile of mutual humour, and then David shook his head ruefully. 'Try not to be late for the meeting,' he advised. 'From the way Mrs Carlson was acting he sounds pretty awesome.'

Leonie grimaced. 'Are you sure you want to

send me, I could walk in, trip over a matchstick, and end up sliding across his desk into his lap!'

'He asked for you specifically.' But David frowned as he mentally envisaged the scene she had just described. 'I'll take the risk,' he said without enthusiasm.

'Sure?'

'No,' he answered with complete honesty. 'But short of lying to the man I don't know what else I can do. Just try not to be late,' he warned again.

And she did try, she tried very hard, but it seemed the fates were against her from the start. She caught her tights on the door as she got into her VW, drove around for another ten minutes trying to find somewhere to park so she could buy some new ones, getting back to the car just in time to personally accept her parking ticket from the traffic warden, making a mad dash to find somewhere to change her tights, laddering that pair too in her haste, although it was high enough up her leg not to show. By this time she in no way resembled the coolly smart young woman who had left Stevenson Interiors in plenty of time to reach Thompson Electronics by four o'clock. It was already five to four, and she was hot and sticky from her exertions with the tights, her make-up needing some repair, her hair having lost its glowing bounce in the heat of the day. She was already going to be a few minutes late; taking time to refresh her make-up and brush her hair wasn't going to make that much difference now.

It was ten minutes past four when she entered the Thompson building, her slim briefcase in her hand, and except for the fact that she was late, looking like a self-contained young executive. Ten minutes wasn't so bad, she could blame that on the traffic. She certainly didn't intend going into the story of the ripped tights as her excuse, or the parking ticket either! It was——

Oh no, she just didn't believe this, it couldn't be happening to her! But she knew that it was as the smooth-running lift made a terrible grinding noise and shuddered to a halt somewhere between the eighth and ninth floors. She was stuck in a lift for the second time that day! And as usual she was alone. She was always alone when the damned things broke down, never had anyone to help calm the panic that she felt. This was a large lift, not like the one at Stevenson Interiors, but she would still rather be on the other side of those steel doors. Oh well, at least the floor was carpeted if she had to spend any amount of time here, so she could be comfortable. But it wasn't likely that she would be here for long, this was a big and busy building, someone was sure to realise sooner or later that one of the lifts was stuck between floors. And she hoped it was sooner!

She sank to the floor after pressing the emergency button, knowing from experience that people rarely took notice of that bell. God, what a day it had been, worse than her usual string of mishaps. If she didn't know better she would think——But no, she wouldn't even think about him. God, this was a hell of a place to start thinking of the disastrous effect her husband had had on her, his disapproval of almost everything she did making her more nervous, and consequently more klutzy, than ever.

She determinedly opened her briefcase, going through the fabric book she had brought with her, wondering what sort of colour scheme the President of the company would favour. She had thought of a few ideas, but basically she just wanted to hear what his tastes were.

She became so engrossed in matching paints and fabrics, the books strewn over the floor, that for some time she managed to forget she was marooned in a lift eight-and-a-half floors up. It was almost five-thirty when she heard the sound of banging from above, a voice that sounded strangely hollow calling down that the lift would be working shortly.

Leonie stood up, her legs stiff from where she had been sitting on the floor for over an hour, losing her balance as the lift began moving almost immediately, jerking for several feet before moving smoothly, Leonie flung about in the confined space, falling to the ground in a sprawled heap as it shuddered to a halt and the door miraculously creaked slowly open.

The first thing Leonie saw from her floor-level view was a pair of well-shod feet, the man's black shoes made of a soft leather, a meticulous crease down the centre of the grey trouser legs. Before she could raise her gaze any further Mrs Carlson was rushing into the lift to help her to her feet, the black shoes and grey-covered legs turning away.

'Bring her into my office as soon as you've helped her tidy up,' ordered a curt male voice.

Leonie turned sharply to look at the man as the other woman fussed around her, but all she saw was the back of the man's head as he entered a room at the end of the corridor.

'Have you been in here long?' The middle-aged woman helped her pick up her sample books from the floor, a tall capable woman who had been secretary to the last President of the company for over twenty years. Leonie had met

her when she worked here last, and although the
other woman tried to be distant and authoritative,
her warm brown eyes belied the role.

Leonie liked the other woman, but she wasn't
sure she liked anyone seeing her sprawled on the
floor in that undignified way. 'An hour or so,' she
dismissed distractedly, pushing the books into
her briefcase, anxious to get out of the lift.

Stella Carlson followed her out into the
corridor. 'In all the years I've worked here I've
never known any of the lifts break down before,'
she shook her head.

Leonie grimaced, brushing her skirt down. 'I
have a strange effect on lifts.'

'Really?' the other woman frowned. 'Well as
long as you're all right now . . .?'

'Fine,' she nodded dismissively. 'I'm too late
for my meeting, so perhaps you could explain the
reason for my delay to your boss and I could
make another appointment for tomorrow?'

'Didn't you hear, you're to go in as soon as you
feel able to.'

She thought of the man with the black shoes
and grey trousers. '*That* was the new President of
the company?' she dreaded the answer, although
she knew what it was going to be.

'Yes,' Mrs Carlson confirmed.

Oh David, Leonie mentally groaned, I didn't
trip and slide across his desk into his lap, but I
did lie sprawled at his feet on the floor of a lift
that *never* broke down! David would never
understand, things like this just didn't happen to
him. They didn't happen to *any* normal person!

'Now seems as good a time as any,' she said
dully, knowing her dignity was past redemption.
'I'm sure I've delayed you long enough already.'

'Not at all,' the other woman assured her as

they walked side by side down the corridor. 'Things have been a little—hectic, here the last few weeks.'

The new boss was obviously giving the employees a shake-up, Leonie thought ruefully, her humour leaving her as she realised she would probably be in for the same treatment. After all, if she hadn't been ten minutes late in the first place she wouldn't have been in the lift when it broke down. Or would she? As she had told Mrs Carlson, she had a strange effect on lifts. She had a strange effect on most inanimate objects, things just seemed to happen to them whenever she was around.

She smoothed her skirt down as Mrs Carlson knocked on the office door, unaware of the fact that her hair was sadly in need of brushing after her fall, that the fullness of her mouth was bare of lipgloss where she had chewed on her lips as she looked through the sample books. Not that she would have worried too much about it if she had known; she couldn't possibly make a worse impression than she had as she grovelled about the lift floor!

Mrs Carlson opened the door after the terse instruction from within for them to enter. 'Miss Grant, sir,' she introduced quietly.

Leonie stared at the man seated behind the desk, the man that belonged to the black shoes and grey legs, the rest of the dark grey suit as impressive, the waistcoat taut across his flat stomach, the tailored material of the jacket stretched across widely powerful shoulders, the white shirt beneath the suit making his skin look very dark.

But it was his face that held her attention, a harshly attractive face, his chin firm and square, the sensuality of his mouth firmly controlled, his nose long and straight, ice-grey eyes narrowed on her beneath darkly jutting brows, silver threading the darkness of his hair at his temples and over his ears. Anyone who was in the least familiar with the businessworld would recognise Adam Faulkner from his photographs in the newspapers, one of the most successful—and richest—men in England today. He was also——

'Miss Grant,' he stood up in fluid movements, the coldness instantly gone from his eyes, his voice warm and friendly, his hand enveloping hers in a grip that was pleasantly warm, not too firm and not too loose; the exactly right handshake for a businessman to instil confidence in the person he was dealing with.

But why he should waste his time on such a gesture with her was beyond her, she was——

'I hope your unfortunate delay in our lift hasn't disturbed you too much,' he continued smoothly, releasing her hand slowly, leaving the imprint of his touch against her flesh.

Leonie was stunned at his obvious concern. 'I—I have that effect on lifts,' she mumbled the same lame excuse she had given Mrs Carlson, conscious of the other woman still standing in the room with them.

Dark brows rose questioningly. 'That sort of thing happens to you often?'

Colour heightened her cheeks. 'Yes,' she bit out. 'Look, I don't think——'

'Don't worry, I'm not expecting you to conduct our business meeting after your ordeal in the lift,' he assured her. 'I suggest we make another appointment for tomorrow,' he looked at Mrs Carlson for confirmation. 'Some time in the afternoon,' he instructed as she left the room to consult his appointment book.

'Please, I——'

'Please sit down, Miss Grant,' Adam Faulkner instructed when he saw how pale she had become. 'Let me get you a drink. Would you like tea or coffee, or perhaps something stronger?' He pressed a button on his desk to reveal an extensive array of drinks in the cabinet situated behind Leonie.

Leonie just kept staring at him, too numb to even answer.

'Something stronger, I think,' he nodded derisively at her lack of response, striding across the room to pour her some whisky into a glass. 'Drink it down,' he instructed her firmly as she made no effort to take the glass from his lean fingers.

She took the glass, swallowing without tasting, reaction definitely setting in.

Adam Faulkner moved to sit on the edge of his desk in front of her, dangerously close, the warmth of his maleness seeming to reach out and engulf her. 'Terrible experience, getting caught in a stationary lift.' He took the empty glass from her unresisting fingers, seeming satisfied that she had drunk it as instructed. 'I've been caught in several myself in the past,' he added dryly. 'Although not lately.'

'It's my second time today,' Leonie mumbled dully, feeling the alcohol in her bloodsteam, remembering too late that she hadn't had any lunch, that the piece of dry toast she had eaten for breakfast wasn't enough to stop the effect the whisky was having on her. That was all she needed to complete her day, to be roaring drunk in front of this man! 'The one at work has always been unreliable,' she added in defence of her clumsiness in getting stuck in two lifts that had broken down.

'Maybe you have too much electricity in your body,' Adam Faulkner suggested softly. 'And it has an adverse effect on other electrical things.'

She looked up at him sharply, and then wished she hadn't as a wave of dizziness swept over her. She was going to get up out of this chair to make a dignified exit and fall flat on her face, just to *prove* what an idiot she was! If this man weren't already aware of that!

'Maybe,' she nodded, swallowing in an effort to clear her head, having a terrible urge to start giggling. In one part of her brain she could logically reason that she had little to giggle about, and in another she just wanted to start laughing and never stop. There was so much about this situation that was funny.

'Miss Grant?'

She frowned up at him. 'Why do you keep calling me that?'

He shrugged. 'It's your name, isn't it?'

'Leonie Grant, yes,' she nodded in exaggerated movements. 'I—Hic. I—Hic. Oh *no*,' she groaned her humiliation as her loud hiccups filled the room. She really was making a fool out of herself—more so than usual, if that were possible! She should never have got out of bed today, should have buried her head beneath the bedclothes and stayed there until fate decided to be kind to her again. If it ever did, she groaned as she hiccuped again.

'Maybe the whisky was a bad idea,' Adam said in amusement, going over to the bar to pour her a glass of water.

Leonie gave him a look that spoke volumes before swallowing the water, almost choking as a hiccup caught her mid-swallow, spitting water everywhere, including over one black leather shoe as Adam Faulkner's leg swung in front of her as he once again sat on the edge of his desk. 'Oh dear,' she began to mop at the shoe with a tissue from her bag, becoming even more agitated when several pieces of the tissue stuck to the wet surface.

She closed her eyes, wishing the scene would evaporate, that she would find it had all been a bad dream. But when she opened her eyes again the black shoe dotted with delicate yellow tissue was still there, and the man wearing the shoe was beginning to chuckle. Leonie looked up at him dazedly, liking the warmth in his eyes, the way they crinkled at the corners as he laughed, a dimple appearing in one lean cheek, his teeth very white and even against his tanned skin.

Mrs Carlson entered the room after the briefest knock, breaking the moment of intimacy. 'I've checked your appointment book, Mr Faulkner, and you're free at twelve o'clock or three o'clock.'

'Twelve o'clock, I think,' he still smiled. 'Then Miss Grant and I can go out to lunch afterwards.'

'Oh but I——'

'Book a table, would you?' He cut across Leonie's protest, smiling at his secretary, much to her obvious surprise. 'My usual place. And you may as well leave for the evening now, Miss Grant and I are just going to dinner.'

'Er—yes, Mr Faulkner.' The older woman gave Leonie a curious look, seeming to give a mental shrug before leaving the room.

'She's wondering why you could possibly want to take me to dinner,' Leonie sighed, wondering the same thing herself. But at least the suggestion had stopped her hiccups!

Adam stood up after dusting the tissue from his shoe. 'It's the least I can do after your ordeal in the lift.'

'But that was my fault——'

'Nonsense,' he humoured.

Leonie blinked at the determination in his face. 'Why should you want to take me out to dinner?'

'Miss Grant——'

'Will you stop calling me that!'

'Would you prefer Leonie?' he queried softly, locking his desk drawers and picking up his briefcase in preparation for leaving for the evening.

'Yes,' she snapped.

'Then you must call me Adam,' he invited huskily.

'I'm well aware of your name,' she bit out impatiently. The whisky may have gone to her head but she wasn't that drunk! And she had no idea why this man should want to take her out to dinner, they——

'Then please use it,' he urged, as his hand on her elbow brought her to her feet.

Leonie swayed slightly, falling against him, flinching away from the hard warmth of his body. 'Please, I don't want to go out to dinner,' she protested as he propelled her from the room at his side, the top floor of the building strangely in silence, Mrs Carlson having followed his instruction and left for the evening, the other employees having left some time ago.

Adam didn't release her arm. 'When did you last eat?' he asked pointedly as she swayed again.

'I had some toast for breakfast this morning. I need to diet,' she defended heatedly as the grey eyes looked her over disapprovingly.

'You're too thin,' he stated bluntly.

'I'm a size ten,' she told him proudly.

'Definitely too thin,' he repeated arrogantly. 'I

happen to be one of those men who prefers his woman to have some meat on her bones.'

His woman? *His* woman! Just who did he think he was? 'I happen to like being thin,' she told him irritably.

He arched dark brows. 'Do you also like starving to death?' he drawled.

It was her weakness for good food that had pushed her up to a size fourteen in the past, and she had no intention of giving in to that weakness again, not when it had taken so much effort to lose the excess weight. 'I'll survive,' she muttered.

'Will you be okay in the lift now that it's working properly?' Adam asked as the lift doors opened to them invitingly.

'I'll be fine,' she dismissed his concern. 'Although the way today is going so far it could break down on us again,' she said ruefully.

Adam smiled down at her as they were confined in the lift together. 'I can't think of anyone I would rather be stuck in the lift with,' he said throatily.

Leonie gave him a sharp look, expecting sarcasm but finding only warm invitation in the dark grey eyes. He was flirting with her, actually *flirting* with her!

'Pity,' he drawled as they arrived safely on the ground floor, stepping into the carpeted reception area, nodding to the man on night security, guiding Leonie to the parking area, opening the passenger door of the sporty BMW for her, the top to the pale blue car back in the heat of the day. He took her briefcase from her and threw it in the back with his own before climbing in next to her, starting the engine with a roar. 'Would you like the top up or down?' he enquired politely.

She touched her hair ruefully. 'I think it's beyond redemption, so down, please.'

Adam glanced at her as he drove the car towards the exit. 'You have beautiful hair.'

Leonie tensed at the unexpected compliment, her breath held in her throat.

'The style suits you,' he added softly.

The tension left her in a relieved sigh. 'Thank you.'

Conversation was virtually impossible as they drove to the restaurant, although the fresh air did clear Leonie's head somewhat, giving her time to wonder what she was doing on her way to dinner with this man. She should have been more assertive in her refusal, shouldn't have allowed herself to be manoeuvred in this way. And yet she knew she was curious, couldn't think what possible reason Adam had for wanting to take her out to dinner. And his tolerance with the mishaps that just seemed to happen to her was too good to last!

She had been to the restaurant before that he took her to, but it had been a year ago, and hopefully no one would remember that she was the woman who had tripped on her way back from powdering her nose and pushed some poor unfortunate diner's face into his dinner!

'Good evening, Mr Faulkner,' the maitre d' greeted warmly, his eyes widening warily as he saw his companion. 'Madam,' he greeted stiffly.

He remembered her! It had been over a year ago now, and this man still remembered her. He probably didn't have many people who came here and assaulted another diner for no reason!

'Do we have to eat here?' she demanded of Adam in desperation as they followed the other man to their table.

His brows rose. 'You don't like the restaurant? Or perhaps the French cuisine isn't to your liking?'

'I love it,' she sighed. 'I just don't feel— comfortable here, that's all,' she mumbled.

'Thanks, Henri,' Adam dismissed the other man, pulling out her chair for her himself. 'Just relax, Leonie.' His hands were warm on her shoulders as he leant forward to speak softly in her ear, his breath gently ruffling her hair.

She felt strangely bereft when he removed his hands and went to sit opposite her, their table in a quietly intimate part of the restaurant. As the waiter poured the wine that had been waiting for them, she could feel the tingling of danger along her spine, wary of this romantic setting, wary of this game Adam was playing with her.

'Adam——'

'Try the wine,' he urged huskily.

'When are we going to discuss the work on your office suite?' she asked determinedly.

'Tomorrow. Before lunch.'

'About lunch——'

'Don't worry, I'm sure you'll like the restaurant I've chosen for us,' he sipped his own wine. 'Please try it,' he encouraged throatily.

She sighed her impatience, ignoring the glass of wine. 'Why are you doing this?'

'This?' he prompted softly.

She shrugged. 'The charm, the restaurant, dinner, the wine. Why, Adam? And don't say to atone for the lift breaking down with me in it because I won't believe you.'

'You're right,' he nodded, perfectly relaxed as he leant back in his chair, dismissing the waiter as he arrived to take their order. 'I had this table booked for us tonight before I even realised you were stuck in the lift.'

'Why?'

'Don't you usually go out for business meals with your prospective clients?'

'Of course,' she sighed. 'But it's usually lunch, and so far we haven't discussed any business.'

'We will,' he promised. 'Tomorrow.'

'Why not now?'

He shrugged at the determination in her face. 'Maybe after we've eaten,' he compromised.

This time he didn't wave the waiter away when he came to take their order, and with the arrival of their first and consequent courses there wasn't a lot of time for conversation. And by the time they got to the coffee stage of their meal Leonie had to admit that she didn't give a damn if they ever discussed business, feeling numb from the head down, the wine one of her favourites, her glass constantly refilled as soon as she had taken a few sips, the food as delicious as she remembered, forgetting her diet for this one night.

'You look like a well-fed cat,' Adam eyed her appreciatively.

'I feel like a *very* relaxed one, if you know what I mean,' she smiled happily.

He grinned. 'I know exactly what you mean.'

He was so handsome, so ruggedly good looking, that he made her senses spin. Or was that the wine? No, she was sure it was him. And he had been so patient with her when she knocked a glass of wine all over the table, had dismissed the anxious waiter to mop up the surplus liquid himself, had got down on the floor and helped her pick up the contents of her handbag when she accidentally opened it up the wrong way and it all fell out, had even chuckled a little when she knocked the waiter's arm and ended up with a potato in her lap. Yes, he had been very charming.

'Shall we go?' he suggested throatily as she smiled dreamily at him.

'Why not?' She stood up, narrowly avoiding another table as she turned too suddenly. 'I never go back to the same place twice if I can avoid it,' she assured him happily.

'It must be difficult finding new restaurants,' he smiled, a smile that oozed sensuality.

'I rarely eat out,' she dismissed. 'It's safer that way, for other diners, I mean,' she explained as they went outside, surprised to see it was already dark, a glance at her watch telling her it was almost ten o'clock. They had been in the restaurant hours!

His mouth quirked. 'I noticed you have a tendency to—well, to——'

'Drop things, knock things, bump into things,' she finished obligingly. 'My husband found it very irritating,' she added challengingly.

'Really?' Adam sounded non-committal.

'Yes. He—Where are we going?' she frowned as she realised they were in a part of London she didn't know very well, the exclusive residential area.

'My apartment.'

Leonie blinked as they entered the underground car-park. 'You live here?' she frowned.

'Since my separation,' he nodded, coming round to open her door for her.

Things were happening too fast, much too fast she realised as they entered the spacious apartment, barely having time to notice its elegant comfort before Adam swept her into his arms, his eyes glittering darkly with desire.

'I've wanted to do this ever since the lift doors opened and I saw you grovelling about on the floor,' he announced raggedly before his mouth claimed hers.

She wanted to ask him what he found so romantic about a woman making a fool of herself, but the magic of his kiss put all other thoughts from her mind, drawing her into him with the sensuous movement of his mouth, his arms beneath the jacket of her suit, his hands warm through the thin material of her blouse and camisole, his thighs hardening against her as his hands moved down to cup her buttocks and pull her into him.

The effects of the brandy and wine miraculously disappeared to be replaced by something equally as heady, sexual pleasure. She had heard all the old clichés about women who were no longer married, had scorned the idea of falling into that sexual trap herself knowing how little pleasure she had found in her marriage bed, and yet she knew that she wanted Adam. And he wanted her, there could be no doubting that.

Her lips parted beneath the assault of his tongue, knowing it was merely a facsimile of the lovemaking they really wanted, Leonie feeling filled and possessed by that moist warmth, drawing him deeper into her as she returned the attack.

Adam's breathing was ragged as he pulled away to kiss her throat, peeling the jacket expertly from her shoulders, throwing it to one side, beginning to release the buttons to her blouse, his hands sure in their movements, although they trembled slightly with anticipation.

It was this slight crack in his supreme self-confidence that encouraged Leonie to do some undressing of her own, his own jacket joining hers on the floor, his waistcoat quickly following, her fingers hesitating at the buttons of his shirt.

'Please,' he encouraged achingly.

Her own hands shook as she revealed the muscled smoothness of his chest, the dark hair there silvered with grey. He was beautiful without the trappings of the successful business-man, wearing only tailored trousers now, his arousal barely contained.

'Leonie!' His mouth captured hers again as she caressed his bared chest, moving fiercely against her, pulling her into him as the tip of her tongue tentatively caressed his lips.

They left a trail of clothes to the bedroom, both naked by the time they lay down together on the bed still kissing, Adam's hands at her breasts making her gasp with pleasure, the nipples hardening and aching, asking for the tug of his mouth. They didn't have to wait long.

Leonie didn't stop to question her complete lack of inhibitions, inhibitions that had made her marriage such an agony, only knowing that this man, with his gentle caresses, held the key to her sensuality in his hands.

Adam kissed every inch of her body, found pleasure in the secret places no other man had ever known, making her tremble uncontrollably as his tongue rasped the length of her spine to her nape, quivers of excitement making her arch back into him as he homed in on the sensitive flesh there.

She lost all lucidity as Adam's caresses brought her again and again to the edge of a fulfilment she had never known, as he always pulled her back from the edge before she could reach the pinnacle she craved, her movements beneath him becoming more and more desperate as he refused to let her escape him even for a second.

'Please, Adam. Please!' Her eyes were wild as she looked up at him.

'*You* take me,' he encouraged raggedly, his eyes black with desire.

'What——?' But she understood what he meant even as he pulled her above him, going to him eagerly, gasping as he lowered her on to him, filling her in every way possible before bringing her mouth down to his.

It was so right that it should be this way, that he should allow her the freedom to be the one to choose their pleasure, a pleasure she had never known during her marriage.

She was heady with delight, kissing the dampness of his salt-tasting shoulders and throat, quivering her own satisfaction as he groaned at the invasion of her tongue, feeling his movements quicken beneath her as he could hold back no longer, the hardness of him stroking her own desire until she felt the explosion begin in the depths of her being, beginning to shake as the warm aching pleasure ripped through her whole body in a climactic holocaust.

'My beautiful Leonie,' Adam gasped as he reached the summit of his own pleasure, exploding in a warmth of warm moistness. 'I knew it could be this way between us!'

And it hadn't stopped there, their strength and desire returning within minutes, their second lovemaking even more intense than the first, the pleasure seeming never-ending.

Leonie looked again at the face of the man who slept beside her, wondering what on earth she had done. Oh God, what had she done!

He stirred slightly as she moved from beneath

the curve of his arm, her movements stilling until she realised he was still sleeping. She blushed as she found her clothes scattered in a disorganised path from the bedroom to the lounge; she had never been so carried away by passion before. She hastily began to dress.

'What do you think you're doing?'

She balked only slightly in the movement of pulling the camisole over her head. 'What does it look like I'm doing?' she said sourly; at least he had had the decency to put on a brown towelling robe before following her from the bedroom!

'Isn't it usual to spend the whole night in circumstances like these?' he drawled, his dark hair still tousled, his jaw in need of a shave now. 'I didn't expect you to go sneaking off while I was asleep!'

'I wasn't sneaking off,' she told him resentfully. 'And there's nothing *usual* about these circumstances!' She tucked her blouse into the waistband of her skirt.

'I want you to stay the night.'

She shot him an angry glare, resentful that he could look so at ease, his hands thrust casually into the pockets of his robe, his stance relaxed. 'Why?'

His mouth twisted. 'I'm sure I've just shown you two very good reasons why.'

'Sex!'

'And what's wrong with that?' He arched dark brows.

'Nothing, you know I enjoyed it,' she snapped, knowing it would be useless to deny it, brushing her hair with angry movements, whether at Adam or herself she wasn't sure.

'So stay,' he encouraged softly.

'I can't, Adam,' she sighed impatiently. 'I

don't know what game you've been playing with me this evening——'

'A game you were quite happy to go along with,' he reminded gently.

She shook her head in self-condemnation. 'It seemed the easy way out at the time, so much easier for me to be Leonie Grant and you to be Adam Faulkner,' she said shakily.

He shrugged broad shoulders. 'Why not, that's who we are.'

'Because until our divorce becomes final I'm still officially Leonie Faulkner, your wife, and you're my husband!'

'And now I'm your lover,' he gave a slow smile of satisfaction. 'It was your idea, Leonie, you're the one that said we shouldn't have married each other but just have been lovers. And after tonight that's exactly what we're going to be!'

CHAPTER TWO

SHE vividly remembered shouting those words at Adam before she had walked out on him and their marriage eight months ago, remembered everything about her disaster of a marriage to this man. And she didn't intend becoming involved with him again in *any way*.

She was fully dressed now, straightening the collar of her jacket. 'Tonight was a mistake——'

'I have another name for it,' Adam drawled.

Her eyes flashed her resentment. 'I'm well aware of the fact that you planned what happened——'

'Don't pretend you didn't want it, too,' he warned her softly.

She blushed at the truth of that; from the moment she had seen him seated across the desk from her at the Thompson building her senses had become alive with wanting him. And the fact that he had acted as if it were the first time they had ever met had added to the excitement. But she had a feeling, knowing Adam as she did, a much less charming and relaxed Adam, that he had realised exactly what effect his behaviour was having on her, that it had been effected to get the response from her she had refused to give him during their marriage.

'It was certainly better than anything we ever shared during our marriage,' she snapped waspishly, waiting for the angry explosion she had come to expect from him when they discussed the failure of the physical side of their marriage.

'I agree.' Once again he disconcerted her; he had been doing it all evening, from the time she had discovered that her estranged husband was the new President of Thompson Electronics, during dinner when he had had such patience with her 'accidents', to the infinite care and gentleness he had shown her during their lovemaking. 'You were right,' he continued lightly. 'We're much better as lovers than as husband and wife.'

'We are not lovers!' She looked around desperately for her handbag so that she might get out of here. 'I've left my handbag in the restaurant,' she finally groaned in realisation. 'And that damned man——'

'Henri,' Adam put in softly, his mouth quirked with amusement.

'He already thinks I'm some sort of escapee from a lunatic asylum.' She hadn't missed his covert glances in her direction during the evening. 'I just can't go back there,' she shuddered.

'You don't have to——'

'And I don't need any of your high-handed interference either,' she cut in rudely. 'Why should one more visit to that place bother me!' she told herself defiantly.

'Because it does,' Adam soothed. 'And there's no need to torture yourself with the thought of having to do it; your handbag is in my car.'

Her eyes widened. 'Are you sure?'

'Very,' he replied with satisfaction. 'You were so eager to get up here that you left it next to your seat.'

'I was not eager to get up here,' she defended indignantly.

'Maybe I should rephrase that,' he said

thoughtfully. '*I* was so eager to get you up here that I didn't give you chance to think of such mundane things as a handbag. Better?' he quirked dark brows in amusement.

It was that amusement that confused her; there had been little to laugh about during their marriage, Adam always so grim. But no one knew the deviousness of his mind as well as she did, and she wasn't fooled by this charm for a moment.

'What are you up to, Adam?' she demanded impatiently. 'Why are you doing this?'

He strolled across the room to her side, his movements gracefully masculine, as they always were. 'I want a lover, Leonie,' he told her softly, only inches away from her as he stood with his hands thrust into the pockets of his robe. 'I want *you.*'

She shook her head. 'You had me for a year, and it was a disaster,' she recalled bitterly.

Adam nodded in acknowledgment of that fact. 'Nevertheless, I want you.'

'You've only just got rid of me!' she reminded desperately.

'Of the marriage, not you, Leonie.'

'It's the same thing!'

'No,' he smiled gently. 'We both found the marriage stifling, the sort of relationship I'm suggesting——'

'With me as your mistress!' she scorned.

'Lover,' he insisted. 'We would be lovers.'

'No!'

'Why not?' his eyes had narrowed, although he remained outwardly relaxed.

'I don't want a lover!'

His mouth quirked. 'You just proved, very effectively, that you do.'

Colour heightened her cheeks. 'That was sex——'

'The best sex we ever had, admit it,' he encouraged.

She drew in a ragged breath. 'Yes.'

'And as I said before, what's wrong with that?'

She sighed her exasperation. 'You just don't understand——'

'I understand perfectly,' he cut in soothingly. 'This has all come as a bit of a shock to you——'

'That has to be the understatement of the decade!'

Adam chuckled, at once looking younger. 'Poor Leonie,' he smiled. 'What's shocking you the most, the fact that we found such pleasure in bed together for the first time, or the fact that I want it to continue?'

She couldn't deny that she was surprised at the amount of pleasure she had known with Adam tonight, a pleasure she had known beyond all doubt that he felt too, his responses open and complete. Their sex-life during their marriage, as with everything else during that year, had been a disaster. Adam had been so experienced that in her innocence she had felt inadequate, and she had resented the way he had tried to control her body, her responses automatic and emotionless, refusing to be dominated by him. But the lovemaking they had shared tonight hadn't been restricted by any of that resentment, had been uninhibited. But that Adam should want such a relationship to continue she couldn't accept, not when the breakdown of the marriage and subsequent separation had been such a traumatic experience for her. They simply couldn't pretend they were two people they weren't.

'The first shocks me,' she replied coolly. 'The

second surprises me. Do you honestly not remember what it was like between us, the bitterness, the pain of knowing we were all wrong for each other from the start?'

'As a married couple, not as lovers,' he insisted forcefully.

'Have you forgotten what *that* was like between us?'

'Didn't this evening prove that it doesn't have to be that way?' he reasoned.

'I'm still the same person, Adam,' she told him with a sigh. 'I'm still sixteen years younger than you are, with the same inexperience—no matter what happened here tonight,' she added pointedly. 'I'm still the same klutzy person I was when we were married——'

'That's a new name for it,' he laughed softly.

'I read it in a book somewhere,' she dismissed impatiently. 'It seemed to suit me perfectly.'

'It does,' he nodded, still smiling, his eyes a warm grey, crinkled at the corners.

'Don't you remember how angry all those "incidents" used to make you!'

'You're right, I was intolerant——'

'You're missing my point, Adam,' she said frustratedly. 'It would take a saint to put up with all the things that happen to me in one day—and that's one thing I know you aren't!'

'Have I been angry tonight at all?'

'That was only *one* night,' she sighed her impatience. 'It would drive you insane—it *did* drive you insane, on a regular basis.'

'Haven't you heard, lovers are more tolerant?'

'Adam!'

'Leonie?'

She glowered at him. 'You aren't listening to a word I've been saying.'

'Of course I am,' he placated. 'You're young and klutzy.' He smiled. 'I really like that word, it describes you exactly.' He sobered. 'As a husband I was rigid and intolerant, lousy at making love to you. As a lover I will be generous and understanding—and very good in bed.'

'In your experience,' she snapped waspishly.

He raised dark brows. 'You sound jealous, Leonie.'

She felt the heat in her cheeks. 'I most certainly am not!'

'It's all right if you are.' His arms came about her as he moulded her body to his. 'From a wife it would sound shrewish, from a lover it sounds possessive. I like that,' he stated with satisfaction.

That wasn't all he liked from the feel of his body pressed so intimately against hers, aroused for the third time tonight. Leonie couldn't pretend not to be shocked by this evidence of his renewed desire; their sex life had deteriorated so badly at the end of their marriage that it was an effort for them to make love once a week; Adam had never wanted her *three* times in one night before!

'Adam, please stop this.' She pulled agitatedly away from him as her own body quivered in reaction to his. 'You've had your fun——'

'It was mutual,' he drawled confidently.

'Not that sort of fun!' she snapped. 'God, I can't believe this is really you proposing this preposterous arrangement! Have you thought of the consequences of your actions?'

'I already know you're on the pill to regulate your periods.' He dismissed the idea of pregnancy.

'Not those consequences!' It was embarrassing how intimately this man knew the workings, and malfunctions, of her body! 'We both have families, Adam, have you thought of their reactions to the relationship you're suggesting?'

'My father and your sister.' The amused glow to his eyes left for the first time that evening. 'I'm thirty-nine and you're twenty-three, do you really think either of us needs their permission?' he ground out.

'Your father hates me.' She deliberately didn't mention her sister's feelings towards Adam, although she was sure they were both aware of those feelings; it had been one of the reasons their marriage had proved such a failure.

'My father doesn't understand you,' Adam corrected gravely.

'There's nothing to understand,' she dismissed scornfully. 'I am what you see. A little more accident-prone around you and your father, but otherwise I'm an open book.'

'Then a few of the pages must have got stuck together, because I never felt that I knew you completely either!' He gave a deep sigh. 'I don't intend to argue about the past with you now, Leonie.'

'Lovers don't argue?' she mocked.

His mouth quirked. 'Only when they know it will take them back to bed to make up.' He took her back in his arms, his mouth claiming hers.

Her lips parted of their own volition, allowing access to the thrust of his tongue, trembling as desire claimed her, clinging to the broad width of his shoulders as she swayed weakly against him.

'Stay tonight, Leonie,' he urged against the creamy warmth of her throat.

She was tempted, God how she was tempted. But she couldn't do it. It had taken her eight months to put herself back together after the devastation of loving this man; she couldn't leave herself open to that sort of pain again.

'No, Adam.' She pushed away from him, breathing hard, knowing by his own ragged breathing that he was as aroused as she was. 'There's something else lovers can do,' she told him tautly. 'They can end the relationship at any time; I'm ending it.' She turned on her heel.

'Where are you going?' Adam asked softly.

'Home!' She didn't even turn.

'How?' his gentle question halted her. 'Your car is still at Thompson Electronics, your keys to the car are in your handbag, your money, too, in case you were thinking of taking a taxi home, and your bag is in *my* car downstairs,' he reminded softly.

She had done it again! 'So much for my grand exit,' she said dully as she turned around.

His smile was sympathetic. 'It really was very good.'

'Don't humour me, Adam,' she snapped.

'Lovers——'

'We are not lovers!' she bit out between clenched teeth. 'And we never will be. Now if you'll give me your car keys for a few minutes I'll go down and get my bag.'

'No.'

'You can't keep me here by force, Adam!' There was an edge of desperation to her voice.

'I don't intend to,' he soothed. 'I'm going to get dressed and drive you home.'

'My car——'

'Will be locked into the car park by this time of night,' he pointed out.

She looked at her wrist-watch; it was after midnight! 'If you will just let me get my bag I can get a taxi home.'

Adam shook his head. 'I can't let you do that this late at night.'

'That doesn't sound possessive, Adam, it sounds autocratic,' she taunted him.

He smiled. 'It's concern for your welfare,' he mocked. 'Lovers are like that,' he told her softly before going back into the bedroom.

Leonie stared after him frustratedly; she should have known that today was going to end as disastrously as it had begun. She should also have known Adam would have something to do with it, had felt a premonition of his presence while waiting to be rescued from the lift, her clumsiness always more pronounced whenever he was around.

She had been too stunned, too conscious of Mrs Carlson's presence, to do any other than follow Adam's lead of it being their first meeting when the other woman introduced them in his office. And once she recovered from the shock of seeing him again after all this time she was too intrigued by his behaviour to do any other than go along with the pretence. And as she had admitted to him, it was easier too. But the pleasant atmosphere of their evening together had seduced her into doing something she would rather forget, something that she wouldn't allow to be repeated, her reaction to Adam totally unexpected, given their history together.

Her breath caught in her throat as Adam returned to the room, the business suit replaced with a fitted black shirt and black cords. Adam *never* dressed this casually!

'Changing your image, Adam?' she taunted to hide her reaction to him.

'Like it?' he smiled, not fooled by her attitude for a minute.

She more than liked it, she wanted him again! It was ridiculous when she had been married to this man for a year, when they had been separated for over eight months, to feel the same instantaneous flood of emotion towards him as she had when she first met him almost two years ago. And yet looking at him now she did feel it, her mouth dry, her palms damp.

'You look very handsome,' she told him primly. 'Now could we please leave?'

'Certainly.' He picked up his car keys.

'Lovers are obliging too, are they?' She couldn't resist taunting as she preceded him out of the apartment and into the lift.

'Any time,' he said suggestively, his body pressed up against the back of hers. 'Just say the word,' he encouraged throatily.

She frowned her irritation, moving gratefully away from him as they walked over to the car, their footsteps sounding loud in the black stillness of the night. Adam proved to be right about her bag, it lay on the floor of the car as he opened the door for her to get in.

'You can pick your car up tomorrow,' Adam suggested during the drive to her home, the car roof up now in the cool of the night.

'Tomorrow?' she frowned.

'When you come for our meeting,' he nodded.

Her eyes widened. 'You don't seriously expect me to still come to that?'

He glanced at her, his brows raised. 'Of course.'

'But I—Wasn't that just a set-up?' she frowned.

'I wanted to see you again,' he acknowledged. 'And it seemed a good way to arrange it in view of the way *you've* felt about seeing me again, but I do also want my office decorated.'

'Not by me,' she shook her head determinedly, quivering at the thought of having to see this man on a day to day basis in connection with her work.

'By you,' he said firmly.

'No!'

'Yes,' he insisted softly. 'I really was impressed by your work on the lower floor.'

'Adam——'

'Yes, Leonie?'

She drew her breath in sharply at his tolerant tone. 'I am not going to work for you,' she told him stubbornly.

'Yes, you are,' he nodded confidently.

'You can't force me!'

'I wouldn't even attempt it,' he assured her mildly. 'But I think you might find it a little awkward explaining to your boss, David isn't it, the reason you won't work for me.'

'You wouldn't make me do that?' she groaned.

Adam shrugged. 'I don't see what else you can do.'

'But David has plenty of other designers, much more capable ones than me!'

'I don't want them,' he stated calmly. 'I want you.'

'Please don't involve my career in this, Adam,' she pleaded desperately.

'All I want is my office decorated, is that too much to ask?'

His innocence infuriated her! 'You aren't just asking *anyone* to do it, I was your *wife!*'

His expression softened into a reminiscent smile. 'I'm not likely to forget that.'

'But I've been trying to!' She was twisted round in her seat as she tried to reason with him. 'I've put my life back together, made the career for myself that I gave up when I married you. I am not about to let you jeopardise that.'

'But I don't want to.' He shrugged broad shoulders.

'You're forcing me into a situation I don't want. You deliberately sought me out for this job, didn't you,' she accused.

He nodded. 'I bought the company because I knew you had worked there once.'

'You—you did *what*?' she gasped.

'Well, I had to have a valid reason for seeing you, I knew you would flatly refuse to go anywhere where you knew I would be.' He shrugged. 'So I bought Thompson Electronics.'

It was an example of the arrogance she had always associated with him in the past; if he wanted something then he went out and bought it. He had once bought her with that same wealth and self-confidence that had blinded her to how wrong they were for each other.

'Then you wasted your money,' she told him tautly. 'Because nothing would induce me to work for you.'

'I didn't waste my money, the company is a very profitable one,' he announced calmly. 'And I don't intend to induce you into doing anything; surely you're adult enough that you could design something for my office suite without letting personalities enter into it?' he raised dark brows.

'It isn't a question of that,' she said stiffly. 'I just don't want to work for you. Wasn't one member of my family enough for you?' she added disgustedly.

'You mean Liz?'

'Who else?' she scorned.

'Liz was the best personal assistant I ever had.'
She had been a little too 'personal' as far as

Leonie was concerned! They had met because of her sister's relationship with Adam, and they had parted for the same reason. 'Look, I'll talk to David tomorrow,' she told him tautly. 'I'm sure he'll be only too glad to send someone else over to work with you.'

'I don't want anyone else,' Adam said flatly. 'I wondered about you and him for a while, you know,' he added softly.

She looked over at him with startled eyes. 'David and I?'

'Mm,' he nodded.

Her mouth tightened resentfully. 'And what stopped you wondering?' she snapped.

He shrugged. 'Your dates were too occasional for them to be anything more than placating the boss who has designs on you,' he dismissed.

Leonie's eyes widened. 'You've been having me watched!' she realised disbelievingly.

'You are my wife——'

'Was,' she corrected tightly. 'We're legally separated, and once the appropriate time has elapsed our divorce will be finalised.'

'I was just seeing if we couldn't speed up the proceedings,' he explained.

Leonie blinked at him for several timeless minutes, unable to believe what she was hearing. 'Are you trying to say you were after evidence of adultery against me?' she said with disbelief.

Adam shrugged. 'I thought you might feel more comfortable about our new arrangement if we were already divorced. I knew that I couldn't wait three years for you.'

'I'm sorry I couldn't oblige!' Somehow the knowledge that he had done such a thing hurt her unbearably. God knows she had enough evidence of adultery against *him*! But she had chosen not to subject any of them to the embarrassing ordeal of revealing their personal lives in public. Knowing that Adam had considered doing it to her made her angry.

'Maybe I should have had *you* followed,' she glared at him.

'Oh, I've been living very quietly since you left me,' he dismissed.

'Quietly doesn't necessarily mean alone,' she snapped.

'In this case it does.'

And she knew the reason for that; Liz had continued to stay with her husband Nick. 'Look, we're getting away from the subject,' Leonie sighed. 'You'll have to have someone else do your work for you.'

'No.'

'Adam, I will not be bullied by you into doing something I don't want to do.'

He held up his hand defensively. 'Have I tried to bully you? Did I bully you into anything tonight?' he added throatily.

Her mouth tightened. Tonight had been incredible, there was no denying that, and plenty of women would be only too agreeable to the sort of non-committal relationship Adam was now offering her. But not her. She had made a fool of herself over this man once, she wasn't going to do it again.

'Admit it was everything you thought it could be,' he encouraged softly. 'No complications of marriage, other people, just you and me making beautiful love together.'

Just talking about the experience made her body tingle. 'But it couldn't stay that way indefinitely,' she reasoned impatiently. 'Sooner or later one of us would expect more——'

'Not me,' Adam assured her with finality. 'I've tried being married to you; it didn't work out.'

She swallowed down the pain his casual admission of their year together caused. It *hadn't* worked out, she would be the first to admit that, but to hear Adam talk so casually about the commitment they had made caused a constriction in her chest, as if someone had physically struck her.

'You?'

'Sorry?' she frowned as she realised she had missed what he had said next.

'You wouldn't want more either,' he shook his head. 'After all, you were the one that ended the marriage in the first place.'

'Someone had to make that decision,' she bit out abruptly.

'Oh don't worry, I'm glad that you did.' He shrugged. 'I'm just not husband material.'

She hadn't thought about that at the time, although perhaps she ought to have done, Adam was already thirty-seven, had had several serious relationships, and even more that weren't serious, and before meeting her he had shown no inclination to marry any of those women, had enjoyed his freedom to the full. It was difficult enough for any man of thirty-seven to suddenly accept the changes marriage made to his life, to a man like Adam, who could have his pick of women no matter what his marital status, it was impossible. And she hadn't known about Liz then either.

'You think you would do better as a lover?' she derided.

'Haven't I?' he quirked dark brows.

She put a hand up to her aching temples. 'It's

late,' she sighed. 'And I'm too tired for this conversation right now.'

'There's no rush.' He turned to smile at her after stopping his car outside the old three-storey Victorian building that housed her flat. 'Are you going to invite me in?'

'Harvey wouldn't like it,' she shook her head.

There was a sudden tension about him. 'Harvey?'

He had been amused at her expense all evening, and now she couldn't resist a little amusement herself. 'Dick wouldn't be too pleased either.'

Adam frowned. 'I didn't know you were sharing your flat with two men.'

'Didn't your private investigator tell you that?'

'No,' he ground out. 'He—What are you laughing at?' he questioned suspiciously when she couldn't contain her humour any longer.

'Harvey's my cat,' she explained between giggles.

'And Dick?'

'Moby Dick.'

'You have a *whale* in there?'

Fresh laughter convulsed her. 'A goldfish,' she finally managed to choke out. 'But I thought the name might deter Harvey from eating him; so far it's worked.'

Adam shook his head tolerantly. 'Klutzy, insane, *adorable* woman,' he groaned as he pulled her over to his side of the car before fiercely claiming her mouth. 'Life has been so dull since you left me,' he rested his forehead on hers as he held her easily in his arms.

'Even a steady diet of caviar can get boring after a while; and I'm *nothing* like caviar!'

'You never, ever bored me; I never knew what you were going to do next!' he smiled.

'That isn't practical for a wealthy industrialist's wife. And I wouldn't stay hidden out of sight as a lover either,' she told him before he could point out that he wanted a lover not a wife. 'Not that I'm considering becoming one,' she added hastily as she realised it sounded as if she were.

'You *are* one.' His quick kisses on her mouth stopped her protest. 'Sweet dreams, Leonie,' he finally released her. 'I'll see you tomorrow.'

She didn't argue the point with him; so far it didn't seem to have got her anywhere. He would find out soon enough that if he really did want his office decorated that someone else would be in charge of it.

'Good night, Ad—Ouch!' She groaned as her hair seemed to be caught on the button of his shirt. 'Adam, help me!' she pleaded, tears of pain in her eyes.

'Sit still, woman,' he instructed with patient amusement, his lean fingers working deftly to free her hair. 'There you go,' he released the last strand, his eyes gleaming with laughter. 'I've heard of giving your lover a lock of your hair, but this is ridiculous!'

'You're the one that's ridiculous,' she snapped, getting out of the car, her exit foiled somewhat as she had difficulty unlocking the door. Her cheeks were red with embarrassment as she turned to speak to him through the open window. 'Good night, Adam. Thank you for tonight, it was an interesting experience.'

His smile didn't even waver at the coldness in her voice. 'One of many,' he promised huskily.

Her mouth tightened before she turned on her heel and walked over to the huge front door that was the entrance for all the tenants of the building. She was aware that the BMW hadn't moved away from the side of the pavement, of Adam watching her, congratulating herself on reaching the door without mishap when the keys fell out of her hand straight into the empty milk bottle standing out on the doorstep waiting for collection in the morning.

For a moment she just looked down at her keys inside the bottle in disbelief. Someone ought to lock *her* up for her own safety and throw away the key!

'Are you all right?'

She turned reluctantly to acknowledge Adam's concern at her delay in entering the building. 'Fine,' she answered brightly as he now stood outside the car, leaning on the roof to look over at her.

How could she nonchalantly pick up a milk bottle and start shaking the daylights out of it! But how could she get in to the building if she didn't? God, she felt so *stupid*.

'Leonie, are you sure you're all right?' Adam sounded puzzled as she still hesitated.

'Yes, of course,' she answered waspishly, trying to unobtrusively pick up the bottle, the keys inside rattling loudly in the still of the night as she tried to furtively shake them loose.

'What on earth are you doing?'

She was so startled by his sudden appearance at her side, having been so intent on her keys in the bottle that she had been unaware of his approach, that she dropped the bottle. Adam caught it deftly before it could hit the ground, looking down at the keys inside.

'Isn't this a strange place to hide keys?' he frowned as he tipped the bottle up and was rewarded by them falling smoothly into the palm of his hand.

Leonie snatched them from his hand. 'I wasn't hiding them,' she snapped. 'I dropped them.'

'Ah.'

Her eyes blazed deeply green as she turned on him. 'What do you mean "ah"?' she challenged. '"Ah, I should have guessed"? Or, "ah, that such an unfortunate occurrence should have happened to me"?'

'Ah, that such an unfortunate occurrence should have happened to you, of course,' he said tongue-in-cheek.

Her movements were agitated as she unlocked the door. 'I wonder why I have difficulty believing you,' she muttered.

'Darling, calm down.' He took her in his arms once more. 'I really don't mind these little accidents that happen whenever you're around,' he soothed.

'I don't remember your saying that the time I caught the bodice of my gown on your father's tie-pin and it took you half an hour to separate us!' She strained away from him, but his superior strength wouldn't allow her to move far, his thighs pressed intimately against hers.

'Dad was the one that was so annoyed, not me,' he reminded with amusement. 'Look at it this way, Leonie, at least he was a captive audience for that half an hour; you always did say he didn't listen to you!'

She looked up at him in surprise; she had never heard him talk about his father so disparagingly before. 'He used to look straight through me,' she said slowly.

'Well he didn't that evening!'

'That gown cost a fortune, and it was ruined,' she reminded him.

'It was worth it just to see the expression on

Dad's face. Every time I thought about the incident afterwards I burst out laughing,' he was grinning even now.

'You never told me that,' she accused. 'I thought I had embarrassed you once again.'

He sobered at the admission. 'You've never embarrassed me, Leonie,' he shook his head. 'You never could.'

She was more puzzled than ever now, some of that emotion showing on her face as Adam let her go this time when she moved out of his arms. 'I have to go in; Harvey hasn't had any supper yet,' she told him in a preoccupied voice.

'You'll have to introduce me to him some time,' Adam straightened. 'I've always liked cats.'

'I didn't know that,' she frowned.

'Maybe you don't know as much about me as you thought you did.'

She was beginning to realise that, she thought as she slowly went up the stairs to her second-floor flat. She would never have dreamt Adam could behave as light-heartedly as he had this evening, that he could laugh at himself as well as his father, that he could find her mishaps so amusing. She had been married to him for over a year, and he was still an enigma to her.

Harvey was sitting on the window-ledge outside when she entered her flat, coming in through the small open window as soon as he saw her, miaowing plaintively.

'All right, all right,' she cut off his reprimand mid-stream. 'You aren't the only one that can spend a night out on the tiles, you know,' she told him as she opened a tin of food for his supper, groaning as she realised what she had said. 'Oh, Harvey, what am I going to do?' She bent down to pick up the bundle of ginger and white fur, burying her face in his side. 'Tonight was so perfect,' she told him achingly.

The cat gave a loud screetch of indignation before jumping to the ground.

'All right,' she snapped at his lack of sympathy. 'I can see you're more interested in your stomach than in my problems.' She put his plate down on the floor, the cat immediately pouncing on it. 'I know you catch mice outside so you can stop acting as if you're starving to death,' she told him crossly, suddenly rolling her eyes heavenwards. 'God, I'm having a serious conversation with the cat now!' She sat down dejectedly in one of the armchairs, oblivious to the passing of time as, his appetite appeased, Harvey jumped up into her lap and instantly fell into a purring sleep, Leonie absently tickling behind his ears as he did so.

Her first meeting with Adam had been totally unexpected. She knew of him of course, her sister Liz having been his Personal Assistant for the last year, but he wasn't at all what she had expected of the wealthy industrialist.

Liz and Nick had been away on holiday for two weeks, still had a week to go, and Leonie was house-sitting for them when Adam paid his surprise visit. The sisters had been close in those days, Liz the senior by eight years, having been like a second mother to Leonie since their parents death three years earlier.

Leonie had opened the door in all innocence that evening, had fallen in love the moment she looked up into that harshly beautiful face, the grey eyes warm, strangely luminous with the black circle around the iris. She hadn't heard a word he said as he spoke to her, having to ask him to repeat himself. He had wondered if Liz were at home even though it were her holiday, had needed to talk to her. Leonie had invited him in as she explained that Liz and Nick had gone away on what they called a 'second honeymoon'.

She had been shy with him, had wished she were wearing something a little more glamorous than an old dress that did little to improve her already plump proportions, her long hair in need of brushing. And then she had cursed herself for the fool that she was, from what little Liz had told her about this man's love-life he was hardly likely to be attracted to a cuddly redhead who barely reached his shoulders no matter what she was wearing!

But Adam had seemed reluctant to leave that evening, even though he knew Liz wasn't there, the two of them talking for hours, until Leonie suddenly realised it was after twelve and she had to go to work in the morning. She had been speechless when Adam asked her out to dinner the next evening.

There had been a week of dinners together, of talking into the early hours of the morning, and each time Leonie saw him she fell a little more in love. Although Adam gave away little of his own feelings, treating her more like an amusing child as he guided her through one mishap after another.

The night before Liz and Nick were due to return home was a magical one, Adam taking her to the ballet, something she loved but could only rarely afford to attend, taking her back to the house he shared with his father. It had been after eleven when they arrived, but even so the lights were on all over the house, the butler greeting them at the door, a maid bringing them a tray of coffee and sandwiches. Leonie had been so nervous she promptly knocked over the plate of sandwiches.

But even that had seemed unimportant as Adam dismissed the incident after helping her put them back on the plate, his eyes almost black as he followed her down on to the rug in front of the fire, his mouth fiercely claiming hers. It was the first time he had done more than give her a polite brush of his lips on hers at the end of an evening, and after her initial surprise at how fierce he was with her she opened her arms and her heart to him.

He could have taken her right then and there on the rug and she wouldn't have cared. But he didn't, his breathing ragged as he pulled away from her.

'Marry me, Leonie,' he had groaned. 'Marry me!'

'Yes,' she gasped her acceptance, on fire for him.

'Soon,' he urged.

'As soon as you want me,' she promised eagerly.

When her sister and Nick returned the next day she told them she and Adam were getting married the following Saturday. Liz had been stunned, and Leonie had thought it was because Liz was surprised at her young sister managing to capture such a handsome and sophisticated man. That was what she had *thought* it was, she should have probed deeper!

Adam had taken over her life from the moment he put the engagement ring on her finger that evening, a huge emerald that he said matched the colour of her eyes. She had been happy with his decision that she give up her job, wanting to be with him whenever he could get home from the empire that consumed such a lot of his time, knowing her career would make that difficult.

She had even agreed to live in the apartment Adam had always occupied at the top of his father's elegant London home. She had agreed to anything Adam asked of her.

Within two weeks of meeting him she found herself married to a man she barely knew and who she was soon convinced didn't know her. Her wedding night was a fiasco, with her acting the frightened virgin that she was despite Adam's understanding gentleness with her. The pain had been incredible, too much to bear, until finally they had to stop. Leonie had huddled miserably on her side of the bed while Adam slept. The next night had proved as disastrous, and the night after that, until the fourth night Adam didn't even attempt to touch her. She came home from their honeymoon still a virgin, too embarrassed to discuss her problems with anyone. Adam had had no such qualms, making an appointment for her to see a gynaecologist and ordering her to attend when she protested. The doctor had taken away all the embarrassment of her problem, had explained that it was something that occasionally happened, and within a short time the problem had been alleviated.

But the damage had been done, and she resisted all Adam's efforts to get her to join in his passion, until finally he lost all patience with her one night, pinning her to the bed as he held her arms at her sides, ignoring her cries for him to stop as he brought her to the peak of ecstasy. After that night he always made sure she had pleasure too, but he always had to fight her first, to break down the barriers of resistance that she had built up against him. In the end he became tired of the fight, hardly ever touching her even though they shared a bed every night.

She tried to make up for her inadequacies in bed by being the perfect wife in other ways, but Charles Faulkner made no secret of his contempt for the young girl his son had made his wife, and she didn't even have Liz to turn to for support, feeling too embarrassed to discuss the failure of her marriage even with her sister.

Her tendency to clumsiness became more pronounced as the months dragged on, so much so that she became nervous of leaving the apartment and going downstairs for fear of earning the derision of Adam's father. It was enough of an ordeal that she had to sit down to dinner with the elderly man every night, usually managing to knock something over. She and Adam had intended eating their meals in their own apartment, but after a week of burnt offerings Adam had decided his digestion couldn't take any more and suggested they go downstairs and join his father for their evening meal. She had been hurt, especially as she was usually such a good cook, but for the sake of peace—and Adam's digestion—she had agreed. It was just another brick falling out of the already crumbling foundations of her marriage.

Adam began to stay late at the office, working he said. They also stopped going out, a way of stopping her embarrassing him in front of his friends, she felt sure. But it just left her more and more to her thoughts of what had gone wrong between them. It was easier to try and find something that had gone *right*. The answer was nothing!

But she decided she wouldn't be a nagging wife, would make the most of the life they had together. Much to the disgust of her father-in-law she had offered to organise the decorating and refurbishing of the house; his reply to that was to call in the most well-known interior designing company in London. Next she tried to take an interest in Adam's work; that was met with blank dismissal. After only a year of marriage she was bored, and she was sure—when she wasn't attempting to break one of the family heirlooms or tipping wine over someone—boring! The marriage had been a mistake, and she knew that even if Adam didn't. She had finally had enough after a solid month of not seeing Adam any other time than when he fell into bed beside her, deciding to go to his office and confront him with the fact that she couldn't go on like this any longer.

She had wondered why Adam's secretary tried to stop her going in to his office, especially after telling her he only had Liz in with him. What she had seen and heard had told her exactly why Adam wasn't even trying to make a success of their marriage, and why her sister had been so stunned that he was marrying her at all!

Adam had tried to reason with her when he followed her home, but she had required only one answer to one question; had he been sleeping with Liz just before they met. His answer made her leave him immediately, telling him that he should never have married her, that if he had only wanted a replacement for her sister then an affair would have been a much better idea—and much less complicated to them all. For that was what she was sure she had learnt when she came upon them unwittingly, Liz in Adam's arms, that their decision to end their affair and for Liz to attempt a reconciliation with Nick, had been a failure. And now they were both trapped in marriages they didn't want. But Liz was expecting Nick's child, couldn't leave him now, and Adam was stuck with her young and klutzy sister.

He hadn't been stuck with her for long, although Liz was still married to Nick, their daughter Emma three months old now. And Adam was proposing that they, Leonie and he, had the affair she had once told him they would be better having!

CHAPTER THREE

'BUT, David,' she protested the next morning. 'I told you how badly everything went.'

He shrugged off her argument. 'Faulkner couldn't apologise enough about your ordeal in the lift. I didn't like to tell him you made a habit of it!'

She had arrived at work this morning all set to tell David how disastrously her appointment with the new President of Thompson Electronics had gone, sure that when he heard all the details that he would be only too glad to put someone else on that job, only to find Adam had already been on the telephone to David this morning, taking all the blame on his own shoulders!

Her pleas with David had been to no avail; he was adamant she work for Adam. And she was just as adamant that she wouldn't, had sworn when she left Adam that she wouldn't take anything from him ever again, and that included this boost to her fledgeling career. 'David, I don't want to work with him,' she told him flatly.

His eyes narrowed. 'Why not?'

She had no intention of telling David that Adam was her estranged husband. Much as she liked the other man, she knew how ambitious he was, and having the wife of Adam Faulkner working for him could give his company the boost into élite London society that he had been looking for.

'I—I don't like him,' she frowned as she knew that was no longer true either. When she had left

Adam eight months ago she had never wanted to see him again, had hated him for his behaviour with her married sister. But last night, the pleasure they had finally shared, giving and taking from each other rather than Adam having to force her response, had changed all that. She couldn't hate a man who had given her that sexual freedom.

Some of the remembered sensuality must have shown in her face. 'Did he make a pass at you?' David frowned.

A pass! Adam had never made a *pass* at a woman in his life! He was much too controlled for that. 'No, he didn't do that,' she answered tautly.

David looked relieved to hear it. 'Then where's your problem?'

'I've just told you, I don't want to work for him!'

'But he sounded very charming on the telephone.'

She grimaced, well aware of how charming Adam could be when he wanted something. He had once wanted her so badly in his bed that he had married her; how ironic that the one thing he had wanted from her had been so disastrous. 'Anyone can be charming for the few minutes of a telephone call,' she dismissed.

'Then he wasn't charming to you yesterday when you did eventually meet?' David probed.

'Yes, he was,' she sighed. 'Very charming.' Colour heightened her cheeks as she remembered just *how* charming he had been later that evening.

'Then why don't you want to work for him?' David repeated again in exasperation. 'I can tell you, he was very impressed with you.'

'I made such a fool of myself,' she said desperately. 'I feel embarrassed.'

David shrugged. 'You always make a fool of yourself sooner or later.'

'Thanks!'

He grimaced. 'But you do,' he reasoned. 'I've never known you to get through a day yet without something going wrong; and it's usually your own fault!'

'That's what I like, a little sympathy and understanding,' she glared at him.

He smiled at her anger. 'Trouble just seems to follow you around. Look, I'll tell you what I'll do, I'll call Faulkner's secretary and tell her I'll be joining the two of you for lunch. If I can see any reason, any reason at all, why you shouldn't work for him I'll put someone else on to it. All right?'

It was the best she was going to get, she could see that. And surely she could make Adam drop the tolerant charm for the few minutes it would take David to realise he would be better sending Gary or Sheila on this job, if only for the sake of his company's reputation.

'I'll drive over with you,' she nodded agreement, feeling a little happier.

David frowned. 'What's happened to the VW, has it broken down again?'

'It's still at Thompson Electronics,' she told him awkwardly. 'Mr Faulkner insisted on driving me home after my ordeal in the lift,' she invented.

David smiled. 'He doesn't know you very well if he thinks a little thing like that will shake you up!'

She gave him an exasperated look. 'Actually, I did some work while I was waiting.'

'See,' he laughed.

She went back to her own desk, her nerves becoming more and more frayed as twelve o'clock neared. Then just as she was tidying her desk in preparation for joining David a deliveryman arrived from a nearby florists. The single long-stemmed red rose took her by surprise, the bold black script on the accompanying card telling her that Adam had in no way changed his mind about where their relationship was going. 'For an interesting experience—one of many', the card read. She crumpled the cryptic message in the palm of her hand, would have done the same with the rose if David hadn't arrived at her office at that moment.

'A new admirer?' He raised blond brows as she thrust the rose into a sadly inadequate glass and pushed it to the far corner of her desk.

She shook her head. 'Another apology from Mr Faulkner.' There was no point in lying about the sender; knowing Adam he would ask if it had arrived!

'Nice gesture.' David helped her on with the fitted jacket to her brown suit, the pale green blouse she wore beneath alleviating its sombre colouring.

'A pity he didn't feel generous enough to send the other eleven,' she said with uncharacteristic waspishness.

David's brows rose. 'I'm sure he—Watch out!' he had time to call out as the sleeve of her jacket caught the perfection of the single red bud, overbalancing the too-short glass, smashing the latter on the floor, the rose crushed among the heavy glass.

Leonie looked down at the ruined perfection with tears in her eyes, instantly regretting what she had done. For the first time in her life she had committed a deliberately destructive act, had knocked against the flower on purpose, not wanting that reminder of Adam facing her when she got back.

'Careful!' David warned as she bent to pick up the crushed flower, sighing his impatience with her as a large jagged sliver of glass stuck straight into the palm of her hand.

Leonie gasped, automatically pulling out the piece of glass, the blood that instantly flowed from the wound the same colour as the rose she still held. She knelt and watched as it continued to bleed.

'You're dripping blood all over the carpet,' David snapped impatiently, taking out a handkerchief to wrap it about her hand, pulling her to her feet. 'We had better get you cleaned up before we go anywhere.' He led her into his office, the First Aid box kept there.

He took the rose she still clutched and threw it in the bin, concentrating on washing her hand and applying a bandage as the small but deep wound continued to bleed.

Leonie felt sick, and not because of the pain in her hand but because of her deliberate destruction of such innocent beauty. It wasn't in her to deliberately hurt anything. Even when she had discovered how Liz and Adam had deceived her she hadn't wanted revenge or retribution, had felt sorry for her trapped sister, although Adam seemed to be continuing with his life as if it had never happened.

'Are you all right?' David frowned at how pale she had become. 'Maybe we should cancel this meeting with Faulkner, you look as if you should go home and rest.'

She shook her head determinedly, not intending to delay this confrontation any longer than was necessary; she had already spent one sleepless night, she didn't intend having any more because of Adam Faulkner. 'I'll be fine,' she insisted, flexing her hand under the bandage; it was a bit sore, but workable.

'Sure?' David still looked concerned.

'Yes,' she smiled brightly, standing up. 'Shouldn't we leave now, Mr Faulkner is going to think unpunctuality is normal for us.'

'For you it is,' David mocked as they went down to his car, a white Cortina that he drove with the usual reserve he had to the rest of life.

The cut on her hand was only a throbbing ache by the time they reached Thompson Electronics, the bandage showing no sign of heavy bleeding.

Mrs Carlson greeted them with a smile, instantly informing Adam of their arrival, ushering them straight in to his office.

'Sorry we're late,' David greeted the other man, their handshakes firm. 'I'm afraid a little— accident, delayed us.'

Leonie hung back behind David, feeling uncomfortable about seeing Adam again. The flesh and blood masculinity of him was much worse than she had imagined after the passion they had shared the previous evening, the royal blue three-piece suit and lighter blue shirt he wore making him look devastatingly attractive, his eyes more blue than grey.

His gaze moved surely past David to her flushed face. 'What did Miss Grant do this time?' he drawled.

Leonie's blush deepened as David grinned. 'A collision with a glass, I'm afraid,' he explained.

'The rose you sent me was in it,' she put in

quickly, challenge in her eyes as she realised he wasn't about to reveal their marital status to David either. 'It had to be put in the bin, I'm afraid,' she added with satisfaction.

For timeless seconds Adam held her gaze, transmitting a message that made the colour burn in her cheeks. 'The rose can easily be replaced,' he finally said softly. 'There's only one Leonie Grant.'

'Thank God for that,' David said thankfully, missing the undercurrent of tension between them, taking the conversation at face value.

Leonie was perfectly aware of the double meaning to Adam's words, her mouth firming frustratedly as she longed to knock that smile off his lips.

'We may as well talk over lunch,' Adam decided arrogantly. 'If that's all right with you?' he consulted the younger man as an afterthought.

'Fine,' David agreed eagerly, seeing nothing wrong in this man taking charge of the meeting.

It was embarrassing how easily David had been taken in by Adam's charm, Leonie thought angrily. He was supposed to be romantically interested in her himself, and yet he seemed to find nothing wrong with the way Adam's fingers closed possessively over her arm as they left the office together, seemed not to notice when Adam moved his thumb erotically against her inner arm.

'What have you done to your hand?' Adam frowned as he noticed the bandage for the first time, his fingers entwining with hers as he lifted her hand for closer inspection.

'She cut herself with a piece of the broken glass.' It was left to David to answer for her, her breath catching in her throat at the intimacies

Adam was taking with her hand in full view of the other man.

Adam's gaze bored into hers. 'Have you seen a doctor?'

She swallowed hard, shaking her head to clear the spell he was casting over her. 'Only David,' she dismissed lightly, putting her other hand into the crook of the other man's arm. 'But he knows how to take care of me,' she added pointedly.

Dark brows met over suddenly icy grey eyes. 'Indeed? You have some experience in taking care of Miss Grant, Mr Stevenson?' the question was put innocently enough, but Leonie could feel the tension in the hand that still gripped hers.

'A little.' Once again David was innocent of the innuendo behind Adam's words. 'I took her to the hospital when she got high using glue in her office one afternoon, and another time when she stuck her letter-opener in her leg.'

Adam's eyes twinkled with suppressed humour as Leonie's ploy to imply intimacy between David and herself failed miserably. 'I wondered how you had acquired that scar,' he said throatily.

Leonie blushed as she remembered the way his caressing fingers had explored the half-inch scar above her knee, how they had explored the whole of her body, pulling out of his grasp to move closer to David. 'He's always rescuing this Damsel in Distress,' she gave David a warm smile. 'I don't know what I'd do without him.'

David looked pleased by her encouragement, having received little enough of it the last six months.

'We'll take my car,' Adam decided abruptly, striding over to the BMW. 'You don't mind if Miss Grant sits in the front next to me, do you,

Stevenson, she gets car sick in the back,' he said smoothly.

David looked surprised. 'I didn't know that.'

Neither did she! But short of calling Adam a liar, and possibly alienating him as a client for David she couldn't very well say so, getting ungraciously into the car next to Adam while David sat in the back. She almost gasped out loud when Adam took advantage of their relative privacy in the front of the car to guide her hand on to his thigh, keeping it there with his own hand when she would instantly have pulled away.

His leg felt firm and warm through the material of his trousers, and she could feel the heat rising in her cheeks as both of them acted as if the intimacy weren't taking place, Adam coolly conversing with the unsuspecting David.

By the time they arrived at the restaurant Leonie's nerves were in shreds, her senses in turmoil as she fought against the desire Adam had deliberately instigated. His gaze was silently mocking as he helped her out of the car, although she flushed as she saw his body wasn't quite as controlled, looking away quickly from the evidence of his arousal, her cheeks burning as they entered the restaurant.

She could see David was impressed by the other man, and the restaurant he had chosen, as they studied the menus. She was going to have to do something, and fast, if she wanted David to take her off this job.

'So,' Adam sat back after they had ordered their meal. 'Is there some problem with Miss Grant coming to work for me?'

David looked disconcerted by the other man's bluntness. 'Problem?' he delayed.

Adam shrugged. 'Does the owner of Stevenson

Interiors usually go to a routine business meeting with his employees?'

'Er—Well—No,' David answered awkwardly. 'But Leonie is rather new at her job. Not that she isn't good at it,' he put in hastily. 'She is. But she—we, wondered if you wouldn't rather have someone more experienced.'

'Just how much experience does Miss Grant have?' Adam asked softly, his hand somehow locating her knee beneath the table, his fingers caressing.

Leonie's mouth tightened at the—to her—unsubtle double-meaning behind the question. 'Not enough for you, I'm sure,' she bit out, drawing in a pained breath as his fingers tightened in rebuke.

'I'm sure you'll satisfy me,' he told her blandly.

'And I'm equally sure I won't,' she grated.

'I'm not a demanding man, Miss Grant,' he drawled. 'I simply know what I like.'

So did she after last night, having explored the hard planes of his body then more thoroughly than ever before, Adam encouraging her to do so, to both their delight.

'I like what you've done for me already,' he continued softly. 'I'd like it to continue.'

Her mouth thinned. 'I don't think I can—work, for you, Mr Faulkner.'

'Leonie!' David gasped. 'What Leonie means is that she does have a couple of other little jobs that need her attention,' he quickly invented. 'And anyway, this conversation might be academic.'

Adam looked at him. 'And why should it be that?'

David gave a nervous laugh at the other man's

quiet intensity. 'Well *I* know we're the best, but I'm sure you'll have other quotes in for the work, and——'

'No other quotes,' Adam told him arrogantly. 'I want Miss Grant to do this for me.'

David flushed with pleasure, and Leonie could understand why. Interior designing was a competitive business, and they lost as many prospective jobs as they won, other companies often undercutting them. If only Adam only had work on his mind!

'In that case,' he beamed, 'I can get someone else to clear up Leonie's odd loose ends.'

'I would appreciate it,' Adam drawled. 'I need Miss Grant right away.'

And he wasn't lying either! His hand had captured hers as she tried to pry his fingers from her knees, guiding it to the throbbing hardness of his thighs. She flinched away from him as if he had burnt her, glaring at him furiously for this subterfuge.

'And, of course, if her work proves as satisfactory this time as last I would consider using her when I have my apartment refurbished,' he added challengingly.

'It's a brand new apartment!' She almost groaned out loud as she realised she had revealed to a shocked David that she had been to the other man's home. 'Mr Faulkner insisted on taking me home to give me a drink to steady my nerves last night before driving me to my flat,' she quickly explained.

'Leonie has a habit of walking into one catastrophe after another,' David smiled.

'I've noticed,' Adam said dryly. 'I feel that my apartment lacks the homely touch at the moment, I'm sure Miss Grant could help me create that.'

She was so angry with him at this moment that if he didn't stop baiting her in this way she was going to pick up his soup and tip it over his head! But maybe if she could show David how Adam kept flirting with her he would realise she couldn't possibly work for the other man; the cold treatment certainly hadn't worked!

'I'm sure there must be a woman in your life who could do a much better job of that than I,' she suggested throatily.

His eyes widened questioningly, and then he smiled knowingly. 'I always think this sort of thing is better accomplished by someone who knows what they're doing.'

She blushed as he turned the innuendo back on her. 'I'm sure you're just being modest, Mr Faulkner,' her voice was husky.

'On the contrary, since my wife left my life has been lacking in a woman's—touch.'

She glared at him in silent rage. And if he really expected her to believe there had been no woman for him since their separation he was insane! Liz might be out of his reach at the moment, but there were plenty of other women who weren't, and God knows he had found little enough satisfaction during their brief marriage.

'How about you, Stevenson,' Adam turned to the other man. 'Does your life have that special woman's touch?'

'I'm not married,' David answered in all innocence, receiving a frustrated glare from Leonie at his candid reply.

'Neither am I—now,' the other man told him in amusement. 'But one doesn't have to be married to have a special woman in one's life.'

David glanced awkwardly at Leonie. 'I suppose not,' he muttered.

'Just as one can have a special woman in one's life even if one *is* married,' Leonie put in with sweet sarcasm, looking challengingly at Adam as his expression remained bland.

'Leonie!' David was shocked at the turn the conversation had taken.

She gave him a scornful look. 'We're all adults here, David,' she bit out. 'And the sanctity of marriage does seem to have lost its meaning to some people. Don't you agree, Adam?' she added hardly.

He shrugged, completely relaxed. 'Divorce has been made too easy,' came his reply.

'Easy?' she repeated disbelievingly. 'You'll excuse me if I disagree!' She glared at him, remembering that she had only been able to be legally separated from him without actually revealing the reason she could no longer live with him, had to wait two years to be free of him.

He gave an acknowledging inclination of his head. 'It seems to me that at the first sign of trouble in a marriage now one of the partners runs to the nearest lawyer rather than trying to work the problem out with the logical person, their spouse.'

If Leonie could have spoken immediately after that arrogant statement she would have told him exactly what he could do with his theory. As it was, by the time she had overcome her rage enough to be able to talk she had also controlled the impulse, conscious of David even if Adam wasn't. 'You believe that's what your wife did, hm?' she prompted hardly.

'Oh no,' he denied easily. 'My wife was perfectly right to leave me, I was lousy husband material.'

Having expected a completely different answer

Leonie was once again left speechless. Adam certainly knew how to disconcert her. And he knew it, damn him.

David coughed uncomfortably, obviously finding the conversation embarrassing.

'You'll have to excuse us,' Adam turned to him with a smile. 'Both being statistics in marriage failure I'm afraid Leonie and I got carried away comparing notes. We'll have this conversation some other time, Leonie,' there was a promise in his voice. 'I'm sure you must have been a much better wife than I ever was a husband.'

Had she been? She doubted it. She had been too young and unsophisticated to cope with the trauma of her honeymoon, had made no effort to bridge the gulf that had arisen between them because of it, had found the physical act between them embarrassing. Then why had last night been so different? Could Adam be right, the lack of a commitment between them made it all so much more uncomplicated, easier to relax and enjoy what they did have?

She looked up to find silver-grey eyes on her, realising he was still waiting for an answer. 'No,' she sighed. 'I don't think I could have been.'

His gaze held hers for long timeless moments before he turned to signal for the bill, breaking the mood, his hand finally leaving her knee as they all stood up to leave.

'So when do you think Miss Grant will be able to start work for me?' he asked David on the drive back to his office, the other man once again in the back of the car, although this time both Adam's hands remained on the steering-wheel; and why shouldn't they, he had no further reason to torment her, he had won. She was going to work for him.

'Monday,' David answered firmly, ignoring Leonie's dismayed expression. 'Is that suitable for you?'

'Very,' Adam nodded, his mouth quirking triumphantly at Leonie.

She glared back at him. 'You will, of course, have to move out of your office once the work begins,' she told him tightly.

'I understand that. But you will be supervising the operation personally, won't you?'

'It's the usual practice,' she conceded grudgingly, knowing that she had to give in, that she had to subject herself to several weeks of working for Adam. But working for him was all she intended doing. If he expected anything else from the arrangement he was going to be disappointed!

'You nearly lost us that contract!'

She had been expecting the rebuke from David ever since they had parted from Adam half an hour ago, but he had remained silent as they went down to the car park to their respective vehicles, had waited until they reached the privacy of his office before turning on her angrily.

'All that talk about not being good enough to do the work,' David continued furiously. 'The man will think I employ amateurs!'

'David——'

'And I could have sunk through the floor when you started talking about the sanctity of marriage. The man's private life is none of our business, Leonie,' he told her disgustedly.

'I——'

'And just how long did you stay at his apartment last night?' he added with a frown.

All colour left her face. 'I—What do you mean?' she forced casualness into her voice.

'The two of you seem pretty familiar with each other's private lives. I've been seeing you for the last six months and yet in one evening that man seems to know more about you than I do!' he accused.

He had given her the perfect opening for her to tell him that Adam was her estranged husband, and yet she couldn't take it. It was much too late for that. The time to tell him had been this morning, before she and Adam acted like strangers for a second time, before David would be made to feel too foolish by the knowledge. He would never forgive her if he was told the truth now.

'I knew you were separated from your husband,' David continued forcefully. 'But I had no idea you were actually divorcing him.'

She shrugged. 'It's the usual conclusion to that sort of mistake.'

'But don't you see, I didn't know,' he said heatedly. 'And yet you told Faulkner after knowing him only a few hours!'

'I—er—Maybe the fact that he's separated too gave us a mutual interest in the subject,' she invented.

'How mutual?' David asked suspiciously.

She sighed. 'Did I seem as if I wanted to see him again, even professionally?'

'No,' he acknowledged slowly. 'But that wasn't just because you're embarrassed about yesterday.'

She stood up, moving restlessly about the room, wondering what explanation she could give David that would sound plausible. 'I think we have a clash of temperaments,' she spoke softly.

'In what way?'

'In every way I can think of,' she snapped. 'I despise everything about the man!'

'Leonie!'

She sighed at her unwarranted vehemence. 'He's a rich playboy who buys and sells everything that he wants and then doesn't want, including women,' she said more calmly. 'I despise that type of man.'

'Are you sure he didn't make a pass at you?' David frowned, still not understanding.

'Yes,' she bit out.

'Disappointed that he didn't?' David sounded puzzled.

Her mouth twisted. 'I don't think that question even deserves an answer,' she dismissed disgustedly. 'Look, I know the type of man he is, David, because—because I was married to one,' she admitted gruffly.

His expression softened at the admission. 'I'm sorry, Leonie,' he said gently. 'I had no idea. If you really think you can't work with the man . . .'

'And how would you explain the change to him after assuring him I was definitely available?' she mocked.

'I could always tell him you broke your neck!'

'Now *that* I'm sure he would believe!' she returned David's smile. 'But I won't have you jeopardise the contract in that way. I'm just being silly, of course I can handle Adam Faulkner!'

There was another cellophane-wrapped box from the same florist laying on her desk when she returned to her office, and she opened it with shaking fingers, this single red rose made out of the finest silk, so delicate it looked as if it had just been cut from the garden. The card read '*This* rose won't be crushed—and neither will I.' Again it was unsigned, but Leonie knew the sender, only too well.

'An admirer?' Gary grinned at her from the doorway.

She sighed. 'You could say that.'

Gary sauntered into the room, a few inches taller than her, with sandy hair and light blue eyes. The two of them had been friends since she first came to work for Stevenson Interiors. He touched the rose. 'He has good taste,' he murmured, looking at her and not the flower.

Ordinarily she wouldn't have minded his teasing, was always refusing the invitations he made her, both of them knowing that he had been happily married for the last five years. But today she wasn't in the mood for his lighthearted flirting. 'It's been a long day,' she said abruptly, turning back to her work.

With a shrug Gary left her to it. Leonie sighed, angry with Adam for upsetting her so much that she had been rude to a man who, although a flirt, had always been kind to her. She stood up to go and apologise to him.

CHAPTER FOUR

'FOILED you, didn't we?' she looked triumphantly at Harvey as he sniffed the silk rose in puzzlement, sitting on the dining-table to eye what looked like a delicious-tasting flower but wasn't. 'You won't be able to chew this one beyond recognition,' she crowed, as with a disgusted tilt of his nose Harvey jumped down on to the floor.

She had brought the rose home with her, too impressed by its beauty to throw it away as she had the last one. And much to her delight she had found that Harvey, who usually demolished any flowers she brought into the house, had no interest in the delicate bloom.

'Out you go,' she opened the window for him. 'No, I'm not going out on the tiles again tonight myself,' she told him as he hung back reluctantly, obviously not intending going anywhere if he was going to be left on his own for hours again. 'Once was enough,' she muttered as she left the window open for him.

She stared broodingly at the rose as she tried to reconcile herself to working for Adam as from Monday. The second—indestructible—rose, had been a warning that he was still intent on having an affair with her. Why couldn't he—She looked up sharply as the doorbell rang, instantly knowing who it was. David was her only, rare, visitor here, and he had gone away for the weekend.

'Adam,' she greeted resignedly as she was proved correct.

'Leonie,' he returned lightly. 'Am I interrupting anything?' he arched dark brows.

'Yes.'

'Oh good,' he walked past her into the room beyond, his denims fitted tautly to his thighs and legs, his black sweat-shirt doing nothing to hide the bulge of muscle in his arms and chest. He looked about the empty flat, his gaze returning to hers. 'I thought you said I was interrupting something?'

'You are,' she closed the door forcefully before joining him. 'My privacy!'

He grinned, thrusting his hands into the back pockets of his denims. 'Nothing is private between us,' he dismissed, looking about him appreciatively.

Leonie tried to see the flat through his eyes, knowing the soft peach and cream decor, and the low-backed furniture and fluffy carpets, wouldn't be to everyone's liking. But it was to hers, was all her own work, and she didn't welcome any comments Adam might care to make.

His gaze returned to hers. 'I think Dad should have let you decorate and refurnish the house, after all,' he drawled. 'Maybe then it wouldn't look and feel like a mausoleum!'

'You agreed with the suggestion when he said he wanted to bring in professionals!' she was stung into accusing.

He shrugged broad shoulders. 'It was his house. But I didn't come here to discuss the past,' he frowned.

'Then why are you here?' she demanded resentfully.

'To take you out.'

She flushed. 'It's usual to ask first,' she snapped.

He shook his head, smiling. 'I knew what your answer would be if I did that.'

'I'm sure you did,' she bit out.

'You'll enjoy yourself,' he promised encouragingly.

She blushed. 'I'm sure I won't!'

Adam chuckled softly. 'Are they very naughty thoughts, Leonie?' he mocked.

'Let's leave my thoughts, naughty or otherwise, out of this,' she said sharply. 'I have no desire to go anywhere with you.'

'Oh yes you do,' he contradicted huskily. 'And maybe later on I just might take you there. But right now I have it in mind to take you skating.'

'Skating!'

'Mm,' he nodded.

She frowned. 'What sort of skating?'

'Well, hopefully, the sort where we manage to stay upright,' he grinned. 'Although I have no objection if you get the urge to fall on me!'

'Adam, have you been drinking?' she looked at him suspiciously.

He shook his head. 'I'm simply acting like a——'

'Lover,' she completed resignedly.

'Exactly. Lovers take their lovers out on mad escapades like this all the time.'

'Who told you that?' she derided.

'I read it somewhere,' he said with suppressed humour.

'You still haven't told me what sort of skating it will be,' Leonie frowned.

'Roller-skating.'

'But I can't roller-skate!'

'Can you ice-skate?'

'No.' Her sense of humour couldn't be repressed any further, not resisting as Adam pushed her in the direction of the hall to get her jacket. 'Can you?'

'Roller or ice?' he quirked dark brows.

'Either!'

'No,' he informed her happily. 'But just think of the fun we'll have trying!'

And they did have fun, Leonie couldn't ever remember laughing so much in one evening in her life before, let alone with the man who had always seemed so rigidly correct to her. Her tendency to be clumsy wasn't so noticeable with everyone else falling over too, in fact she had almost mastered the sport by the end of the evening while Adam still landed in an undignified heap on his bottom most of the time, and that for a man who had always seemed *so* dignified!

This new irrepressible Adam was impossible to resist, laughing at himself and her in a way she would never have thought he could. If this evening was an example of his indulgence as a lover she didn't know how she was going to continue to say no.

'I'm coming in,' he told her when they reached her flat, his expression suddenly serious.

'Adam——'

'I want to look at your hand.'

The statement startled her; it wasn't what she had been expecting at all. 'My hand?' she repeated incredulously.

'Well I'd like to take a look at all of you,' he told her huskily. 'But I think we'll start with the hand. Did you think I wouldn't notice the discomfort it's given you tonight?' he chided as they entered her home.

She had hoped that he hadn't, but she should have known better; Adam noticed everything! Her hand had been aching most of the afternoon but she had put that down to the healing process. The increased pain she had been suffering the last couple of hours seemed to indicate it was more than that, her falls at the rink only aggravating it.

She took off her jacket, holding out her hand for Adam's inspection.

'You may as well sit down,' he shrugged out of his own casual jacket. 'I'm not going for a while yet.' He came down on his haunches in front of her, compellingly attractive.

He was very gentle with her as he peeled off the bandage, removing the gauze dressing to reveal a very red and angry-looking cut. Leonie grimaced as he unbuttoned the cuff of her blouse to show that the redness extended in a line up her arm.

'It's infected,' he mumbled, looking up at her. 'You'll have to go to hospital for treatment, I'm afraid.'

'Couldn't it wait until morning?'

'It could,' he acknowledged softly. 'But why suffer all night when you could get some relief now from the pain I'm sure you must be feeling?'

His logic always made sense, and he was right, the pain was bad; she doubted she would be able to sleep tonight without something to dull the pain.

'I'll just put a fresh bandage on it and then we'll go,' Adam stood up decisively as he sensed her consent. 'Do you have a medicine cabinet?'

'In the bathroom,' she pointed to the appropriate door. 'With my penchant for accidents I'd be insane to be without one,' she added self-derisively.

Adam grinned. 'I know you can't be feeling too bad when you still have your sense of humour. It was one of the things I always liked about you.'

One of the only things, Leonie thought ruefully as he went into the bathroom. The statement had reminded her of exactly who they were, of the fact that they were in the process of divorcing each other; she had been in danger of forgetting that fact with Adam being so boyishly charming.

He was still in the bathroom when the telephone began ringing. God, she had forgotten it was Friday night, hadn't realised it was already eleven-thirty!

'Yes?' she grabbed up the receiver, not in the least surprised when she recognised the caller's voice, giving a mental groan as Adam came out of the bathroom, frowning when he saw she was on the telephone. 'Oh yes?' Leonie answered her caller faintly. 'How interesting. Look, I'm sorry,' she cut in hastily as Adam approached. 'But I can't talk just now.' She slammed the receiver down, smiling brightly at Adam.

He frowned down at her. 'Who on earth telephones at this time of night?' he asked slowly.

She shrugged. 'I remember you did a couple of times during the two weeks before we were married.'

'That was different,' he dismissed.

'Why was it?'

'Because if I couldn't be in bed with you then I wanted to at least talk to you while you were in bed,' he told her absently, his thoughts obviously still on the call she had just taken.

'Maybe my caller felt the same way,' her voice was shrill at the irony of that statement.

'Is he the one that owns the man's razor in the bathroom?'

Her mouth tightened. '*I'm* the one who owns the man's razor in the bathroom,' she bit out resentfully. 'For some reason they happen to be cheaper and easier to find than the so-called women's razors are. And please don't ask why I need a razor,' she glared at him.

His mouth quirked. 'I won't.'

'Then let me say I don't appreciate your prying into my bathroom cabinet. The medicine chest is next to it,' she snapped.

'And the scissors were conspicuous in their absence,' he pointed out softly.

She remembered now, she had used them to cut a broken fingernail, and must have put them back in the wrong cabinet. 'Well I don't see that it's any business of yours even if the razor *had* belonged to a man,' she told him huffily.

Adam shrugged. 'I'm a very possessive lover.'

'You aren't——'

'Just as I expect you to be,' he continued softly, his gaze compelling.

'Being possessive didn't do me much good while I was your wife,' she reminded waspishly.

He shrugged. 'I've already admitted what a lousy husband I was.'

'And assured me you're a fantastic lover!' she derided harshly.

'And very possessive,' he nodded, his eyes narrowed. 'Which means I want to know who would call you this time of night?'

She had hoped to divert him off the subject, she should have realised he wasn't a man to be diverted. 'A friend,' she dismissed. 'I—They work nights,' she added desperately.

Adam frowned. 'Is that supposed to explain why they would call at eleven-thirty at night?'

'It goes on the company's telephone bill?' she suggested with a grimace for her inadequacy at lying.

'Not good enough, Leonie,' he shook his head. 'I want to know——' he broke off as the telephone began to ring again, picking up the receiver before Leonie had a chance to do so.

Leonie paled, knowing that the person on the other end of the line wouldn't realise from Adam's silence that it wasn't her he was talking to. She could guess what Adam's reaction was going to be.

'That's very interesting,' he suddenly ground out fiercely. 'Now let me tell you what I'd like to do to you——' his teeth snapped together as the caller obviously rang off, slamming his own receiver down with suppressed violence. 'How long has this been going on?' he demanded to know.

She pulled a face, knowing she couldn't evade answering him. 'Ever since I moved in here.'

'And how long is that?'

She shrugged. 'Six months or so.'

Adam's mouth compressed into a thin line. 'And is he always so—so——'

'Obscene?' she finished with a grimace. 'I think that's how those sort of calls got their name!'

She knew exactly what Adam would have heard when he picked up the telephone, had heard the same revolting filth only minutes earlier. The first time she had received such a call she had felt so sick she was almost physically ill, had felt so threatened she had moved into a hotel for the night. The second time she had been angry, so angry she called the police. They sent someone round to talk to her, but in the end all they could advise was that she change her telephone number. But the calls had still continued. She still felt sick at the disgusting things he said to her each week, but she no longer felt threatened, was sure after all this time that whoever he was he preferred to violate her over the telephone, that he wouldn't actually come to her home and carry out the things he threatened.

'Have you done anything about it?' Adam grated, the nerve pulsing in his jaw telling of his anger.

Leonie sighed. 'I've changed my telephone number twice, but it's made no difference.'

Adam frowned. 'He got your new number both times?'

She nodded. 'Even though they're unlisted.'

'How often does he call?' Adam's eyes were narrowed.

'Every Friday night at eleven-thirty,' she sighed. 'There's nothing we can do, Adam, and as long as he stays on the other end of that telephone I can cope with it. Actually, he's getting a little boring now,' she grimaced. 'His fantasy seems to be stuck in a groove.'

'I heard,' Adam rasped.

'Interesting idea, isn't it,' she dismissed with bravado. 'I've told him I think we could do ourselves a mischief, but he——'

'Leonie!' Adam cautioned tightly. 'Can't you take anything seriously?'

'I thought you always liked my sense of humour!'

'Not about something like this,' he said grimly, his hands thrust into his denims pockets. 'The man's a damned fruit-cake, how can you make jokes about it!'

'How?' her voice cracked emotionally. 'I'll tell you how! Because every Friday night I live in dread of those calls, and every Friday night at eleven-thirty he calls without fail. In a way it's a relief when he does call, at least then I can relax for another week. You see, I have a theory,' her voice was shrill. 'That while he continues to call he won't actually come here.'

'You think he knows where you live?' Adam frowned.

'I would say it's a logical assumption,' she nodded. 'If he can get my telephone number three times he can certainly get my address!'

'Then you can't stay here,' Adam decided arrogantly.

'Oh but I can,' she told him. 'I thought about moving, but don't you see,' she reasoned at his furious expression, 'I'm as safe here as I can be anywhere. This man obviously has the means at his fingertips to find out anything he wants to know about me. If I move he'll know that too, so why go through the bother of it?' She shrugged.

'Then you can't stay here alone,' Adam told her grimly.

'Are you offering your services as bodyguard, Adam?' she mocked.

'And if I were?'

She shook her head. 'I don't need, or want, a live-in lover.'

'Have you been to the police about this?'

'There's nothing they can do. The man doesn't threaten me, he just talks dirty!'

'He *talks* about violating you!'

'And do you realise how many obscene telephone calls are received and reported each year? I can tell you that it's thousands,' she said wearily. 'The police don't have enough people to follow up on all of them. They asked me all the usual questions, did I know of anyone who would want to do this to me, did I recognise his voice? I don't, and I didn't! It's all I can do to stop myself being sick when he calls. Now can we drop the subject, hm?' she said brittlely.

His mouth tightened. 'I think you should move from here,' he stated stubbornly, his jaw rigid.

'There's just no point to that,' she sighed. 'And except for his telephone calls, which will probably continue wherever I live, I like it here. No, Adam, I'm not moving,' she told him firmly. 'And one of these days he's going to get tired of calling me.'

'And what do you think will happen then?'

'Hopefully he'll leave me alone,' she shrugged.

'Hopefully!' Adam repeated raggedly. 'What if he decides to come here and act out his fantasy?'

She shivered as he put into words what she had tried not even to think about. 'The percentage of those that actually carry out the things they talk about is very low,' she dismissed.

'You could be one of the victims of that percentage! God, Leonie,' he groaned, taking her into his arms as she began to tremble. 'I don't mean to frighten you, but I can't bear the thought of some maniac wanting to hurt you.'

Her face was buried against his chest, and for a few minutes she allowed herself the luxury of leaning against his strength, of feeling protected. Then she moved back to smile at him brightly. 'Maybe the fact that you answered the telephone tonight will frighten him off,' she suggested derisively. 'I'm sure he didn't get the same satisfaction whispering those things in your ear!'

'No,' Adam agreed grimly, shaking off his worry with effort. 'Let's hope you're right. Now we had better get you to the hospital—What the hell was that?' he jumped nervously as there was a noise at the window.

Leonie laughed softly. 'It's only Harvey

wanting to come in.' She moved to open the window for the ginger and white tabby-cat to come inside.

Adam looked at him with relief. 'After that call my imagination is running riot!' he admitted ruefully, bending down on his haunches to stroke the cat's sleek fur as Harvey strolled over to inspect him.

'Stroking a cat is supposed to be good for the heart and blood pressure,' Leonie mocked him.

Adam glanced up at her. 'I can think of another redhead I would rather stroke!'

Leonie gave a rueful laugh. 'I think I walked right into that one!'

'You did,' he straightened. 'Any offers?'

She shook her head. 'I think one lecher per household is enough—and judging by the amount of females that wait outside for Harvey every night he's it!'

Adam laughed softly, his tension momentarily forgotten. 'Bit of a ladies' man, is he?'

'You could say that,' she grimaced. 'I certainly get the impression the cat population in the area could be on the increase in the next few months!'

'Is he going to need anything before we leave?'

She shook her head. 'He's already been fed, he's just home to rest after his exhausting evening out.' She moved across the room to check the wire mesh on top of the goldfish bowl that stood on the sideboard.

'So this is Moby,' Adam stood at her side watching the fish as it swam into the weeds at the bottom of the bowl.

'I think he snubs his nose at Harvey sometimes,' she smiled. 'A sort of "Hah, hah, you can't get me!" look.'

Adam chuckled, helping her on with her jacket,

careful of her aching hand and arm. 'This household is like you; crazy!'

'I like it,' she shrugged.

'So do I,' he said throatily. 'Leonie——' He stepped back as she winced. 'Is your hand getting worse?'

'It's—painful,' she conceded. But not half as painful as the casual way he kept taking her into his arms! He had been doing it all evening, first at the skating-rink, when he took every opportunity he could to touch her, and now, when the situation was much more precarious, her bedroom all too close.

Somewhere during the evening she had lost sight of the fact that they were adversaries, not lovers. After his disgusting behaviour at lunch today she shouldn't even have been talking to him, let alone have agreed to go out with him. Admittedly, with Adam in this irrepressible mood it was a little difficult to remain angry with him, but she shouldn't have actually enjoyed herself! The same problem still applied to any relationship between Adam and herself; Adam's feeling for her unattainable sister still standing between them.

'Shall we go?' she said sharply. 'It's very late, and I have to go out in the morning.'

'Where?'

She looked at him coolly as they went downstairs together. 'I always visit Liz and Nick on Saturday mornings,' she informed him distantly. 'Nick would think it a little strange if I didn't make the effort to visit my niece.'

'And Liz?'

'I'm sure you're well aware of the reason that I find it difficult to be with my sister,' she bit out, coming to a halt as they got outside. 'Thanks for a nice evening, Adam,' she dismissed. 'Even if I didn't quite manage to skate properly.'

'I'm coming to the hospital with you.'

'I'm not a child,' she snapped at his arrogance. 'I'm quite capable of taking myself to the hospital.'

'And driving yourself there?' he reasoned softly. 'With only one hand?'

She blushed at the truth of that. Unlike his own car hers wasn't automatic; she definitely needed two capable hands for driving, and she certainly couldn't use her injured one. 'I can get a taxi,' she insisted.

'As I told you yesterday, not at this time of night you won't. Especially now that I know there's some sex-pervert with his eye on you,' he added grimly.

God, had it only been yesterday that she and this man had shared so much passion! It seemed as if he had never been out of her life, as if they hadn't been separated for eight months, although she knew this was a different Adam from the one she just couldn't live with any more. This Adam had the power of seduction, a power he wasn't averse to using whenever she proved difficult; which was most of the time!

He took complete charge when they reached the hospital, declared himself her husband as he stood at her side and watched as they cleaned her wound, gave her tablets to fight the infection, and others to kill the pain.

Like this he was more like the Adam she had first fallen in love with, and as they left the hospital together she decided to make it plain to him exactly where they stood in this relationship he had decided he wanted with her. 'I accepted your offer to drive me to the hospital, but that's all I accepted,' she told him abruptly.

'Why, what do you mean?' he asked with feigned innocence as he opened the car door for her, quickly joining her as he got in behind the wheel.

'I mean you are not spending the night with me,' she looked at him with steady green eyes.

'Did I ask if I could?'

'Adam,' she sighed. 'I may not live with you any more but I do know that you aren't a man that asks; you take.'

His expression sobered. 'I took because you wouldn't give freely,' he rasped.

'And I wouldn't give freely because the more I gave the more you took!'

'I wanted to make love to my wife, I don't consider that a bad thing. Most wives complain their husband doesn't pay enough attention to them in bed!'

'The sexual act didn't hold the same pleasure for me as it did for you,' she snapped.

'But that's no longer the case, is it,' he reasoned calmly. 'Last night you demanded as well as gave.'

She blushed at the mention of her wanton responses the night before. 'Last night I wanted you too,' she admitted. 'Wanted to know if I could respond to you.'

'And you did.'

'Yes.'

'Then there's no problem, is there,' Adam dismissed.

'Yes, there's a problem,' she told him angrily. 'The problem is *you*, Adam. I can't deny that last night was a success, but I don't want to repeat it. I don't want to work for you, I don't want to be with you.'

'Too bad, the contract is already signed. And

as for being with me, you enjoyed yourself tonight, didn't you?'

She had, she couldn't deny the fun they had had together. 'But it wasn't you, Adam,' she protested impatiently. 'You're the man who owns an empire——'

'Several companies,' he corrected softly.

'It doesn't matter how many,' she sighed. 'You're rich, successful, sophisticated. You aren't really the man that took me roller-skating tonight.'

'Then who was he?' Adam asked her quietly, not expecting an answer.

And Leonie couldn't give him one. The man she had been with tonight, been to bed with last night, was a man she could like all too much. And she didn't want to like him, knew that if she ever came to truly like Adam rather than just have fallen in love with him that she would be lost.

'I'll see you at nine-thirty on Monday morning,' he told her as they parted at her door. 'You're sure you're going to be all right on your own?'

'My hand is fine now——'

'I wasn't thinking of your hand,' he said grimly.

'The telephone calls?' she realised, shaking her head. 'He only ever calls that once, at eleven-thirty on a Friday night.'

And it wasn't until she lay in bed that night, Harvey curled up against her side, that she realised that for the first time since the calls began she hadn't even thought about or dreaded tonight's call, that she had been so fascinated by Adam that she had forgotten all about it!

CHAPTER FIVE

LIZ was as beautiful as ever. No, more beautiful. Since Emma had been born three months ago Liz had possessed an inner glow of beauty that far outshone her obvious physical beauty. Her blonde hair was styled attractively close to her head, kept shorter now for convenience sake, having little time to fuss over her appearance now that she had a baby to care for. Her widely spaced hazel eyes were often more green than brown, glowing with the happiness she felt in her new role, her mouth curved into a perpetual smile, her figure having returned to its previous sylph-like elegance, although she wore little that emphasised that fact, her clothes loose and comfortable rather than fashionably styled as they used to be.

Yes, to an outsider Liz looked the perfect wife and mother, ecstatically happy in both those roles. And if Leonie hadn't seen her four-month pregnant sister in Adam's arms she may even have been fooled into believing that image herself.

But she had seen Liz in Adam's arms, had heard her sobbing about when they had been together. Adam had looked up and seen Leonie's stricken face as she watched them from the doorway, but he hadn't come after her straight away, had continued to hold Liz as she cried. In that moment Leonie had realised what a fool she had been, what fools they had all been to think that any marriage other than with the person you loved could possibly work out.

When Adam returned to the house over an hour later her suitcases were already packed, and she was waiting for the taxi to arrive that would take her to a hotel until she could decide what to do with her life now that her marriage was over, the Porsche Adam had given her when they returned from their honeymoon parked outside the house, the keys left on the dressing-table for Adam to pick up, all of the clothes he had given her still hanging in the wardrobe. She wanted nothing he had given her.

He had tried to reason with her, to explain what she had seen, but she had only one question she wanted answered; had he slept with Liz. The guilt on his face had been answer enough. Not that she could altogether blame him for that, Liz was a very beautiful woman, what she couldn't forgive was the fact that he had involved her in their triangle of misery.

She may have left Adam but Liz remained with Nick, both of them adoring the beautiful child they had created between them. But Leonie couldn't help wondering how long that would last, when Liz would decide she had shared Emma with Nick long enough and went back to Adam. Worst of all she wondered how Nick would react to knowing that his wife no longer loved him, that she had stayed with him only because she was expecting his baby. Nick adored Liz, had been in their lives ever since Leonie could remember, his love for Liz evident in everything that he did.

Leonie watched him now as he played on the floor with Emma, the little baby gurgling up at him, her huge green eyes glowing. Nick wasn't a handsome man, but he was strong, in body as well as mind. Having just passed his fortieth birthday he still remained remarkably fit, his blond hair peppered with silver giving him a distinguished air. He had lived next to them since their parents died, had been ecstatic when Liz accepted his proposal.

Leonie loved him like a brother, wished there were something she could do to prevent the pain and disillusionment he would feel when Liz tired of playing house and decided to leave him. But he was happy now, deserved that happiness after the long wait he had had for Liz; why end that happiness prematurely?

'You'll stay for lunch, won't you, Leonie?' Nick looked up to smile.

'Er—no, I don't think so,' she refused, finding even this two-hour duty visit per week a strain.

He grinned, straightening, Emma in his arms. 'I can assure you that Liz's cooking has improved since she's been home full time,' he mocked.

'Just for that, Nick Foster, I may decide not to cook your Sunday lunch tomorrow,' Liz pretended to be offended, but she couldn't help smiling.

'You wouldn't do that to a starving man,' he protested.

Liz grimaced at him. 'You look as if you're starving,' she looked pointedly at his muscular physique.

Leonie's heart ached at the way Liz was able to banter and share her life with a man she no longer loved; *she* certainly hadn't been able to do the same once she knew the truth about Adam and Liz.

'Your mummy is implying I'm putting on weight,' Nick spoke to his daughter of his indignation at the suggestion.

'She isn't implying anything,' Liz laughed

softly, taking the baby from him. 'She would tell you if you were. I can't have you running to seed after only a few years of marriage.' She began to feed Emma.

There was nothing more natural than a woman with a baby at her breast, and yet the sight of Liz and Emma together in that way twisted a knife in Leonie's heart. She had suggested to Adam that they have a baby, had hoped it might help draw them closer together, to give her the confidence in herself as a woman that she so sadly lacked with the failure of the physical relationship. But Adam had turned down the idea, had told her children didn't fit into his plans for some time to come. No doubt Liz's child would be a different matter!

She wondered if Liz would feel quite so content if she knew that Adam was trying to have an affair with her. Why didn't Liz just go to him now and save them all a lot of heartache! She stood up jerkily, unable to take any more. 'I really do have to go now.'

Liz frowned. 'But you've only just arrived.'

'I—My hand is aching,' she didn't exactly lie, her hand did ache, despite the pain-killers she had been taking to ease that.

'How did you do it?' Liz looked concerned.

She shrugged. 'Just another of my little "accidents",' she dismissed.

Nick gave her a teasing smile. 'I'm glad you've never come to me for insurance, it would be embarrassing having to turn down my sister-in-law as too much of a risk!'

She returned his smile. 'I don't think I could have afforded the premium anyway on my record!'

'You never used to be quite as bad as this.'

A | FIRST CLASS OPPORTUNITY FOR YOU

◆ **Grand Prize** – Rolls-Royce™
(or $100,000)

◆ **Second Prize** – A trip for two to Paris
via The Concorde

◆ **Third Prize** – A Luxurious Mink Coat

The Romance can last forever… when you take advantage of this no cost special introductory offer.

4 "HARLEQUIN PRESENTS®" – FREE! Take four of the world's greatest love stories – FREE from Harlequin Reader Service®! Each of these novels is your free passport to bright new worlds of love, passion and foreign adventure!

But wait… there's _even more_ to this great _free offer_…

HARLEQUIN TOTE BAG – FREE! Carry away your favourite romances in your elegant canvas Tote Bag. With a snap-top and double handles, your Tote Bag is valued at $6.99 – _but it's yours free with this offer!_

SPECIAL EXTRAS – FREE! You'll get our free monthly newsletter, packed with news on your favourite writers, upcoming books, and more. Four times a year, you'll receive our members' magazine, Harlequin Romance Digest®!

MONEY-SAVING HOME DELIVERY! Join Harlequin Reader Service® and enjoy the convenience of previewing eight new books every month, delivered right to your home. _Great savings_ plus _total convenience_ add up to a sweetheart of a deal for you.

BONUS MYSTERY GIFT! P.S. For a limited time only you will be eligible to receive a _mystery gift free_!

TO EXPERIENCE A WORLD OF ROMANCE.

How to Enter Sweepstakes & How to get 4 FREE BOOKS, A FREE TOTE BAG and A BONUS MYSTERY GIFT.

1. Check ONLY ONE OPTION BELOW.
2. Detach Official Entry Form and affix proper postage.
3. Mail Sweepstakes Entry Form before the deadline date in the rules.

H·A·R·L·E·Q·U·I·N

FIRST·CLASS

Sweepstakes

OFFICIAL ENTRY FORM

Check one:

☐ Yes. Enter me in the Harlequin First Class Sweepstakes and send me 4 FREE HARLEQUIN PRESENTS® novels plus a FREE Tote Bag and a BONUS Mystery Gift. Then send me 8 brand new HARLEQUIN PRESENTS® novels every month as they come off the presses. Bill me at the low price of $1.95 each (a savings of $0.30 off the retail price). There are no shipping, handling or other hidden charges. I understand that the 4 Free Books, Tote Bag and Mystery Gift are mine to keep with no obligation to buy.

☐ No. I don't want to receive the Four Free HARLEQUIN PRESENTS® novels, a Free Tote Bag and a Bonus Gift. However, I do wish to enter the sweepstakes. Please notify me if I win.

See back of book for official rules and regulations.
Detach, affix postage and mail Official Entry Form today!

308-CIP-U1AX

FIRST NAME_____ LAST NAME_____
(Please Print)

ADDRESS_____ APT._____

CITY_____

PROV./STATE_____ POSTAL CODE/ZIP_____

"Subscription Offer limited to one per household and not valid to current Harlequin Presents® subscribers. Prices subject to change."

ENTER THE H·A·R·L·E·Q·U·I·N

FIRST·CLASS *Sweepstakes*

Detach, Affix Postage and Mail Today!

Harlequin First Class Sweepstakes
P.O. Box 2800, 5170 Yonge St.
Postal Station A
Willowdale, Ontario
M2N 6J3

Her smile became brittle at her sister's observation. 'No,' she acknowledged tightly.

'I remember Adam always used to have the effect of making you worse,' Nick mused.

'Have you seen anything of him?'

How casually her sister made her interest sound! She had no idea if Liz saw Adam at all, rarely discussed anything personal with her sister, least of all Adam. But she assumed that they would meet occasionally, despite Liz's act of the devoted wife. 'I saw him yesterday as a matter of fact,' she replied lightly. 'He's looking very well.'

'He always does,' Liz observed affectionately. 'Have the two of you—resolved your differences?'

The look she gave her sister was scathing to say the least. 'We never will,' she said dully, knowing Liz must know that above all people. 'Our marriage is over.'

'I'm sorry, I assumed because you met yesterday . . .?'

'I'm going to be working for Adam for a few weeks, nothing more than that,' she dismissed.

Hazel eyes widened. 'Adam has hired you to work for him?'

'Yes,' she bit out. 'I may not be any good as a wife but I'm a damned good interior designer.'

Liz looked taken aback by her bitterness. 'I'm sure you are, it just seems an—odd, arrangement.'

Not half as odd as the other arrangement Adam was suggesting! She shrugged. 'Adam isn't a man that cares how things look. And I have little say in the matter, David decides who will do what.'

'How is David?' Nick asked interestedly.

'Very well.' Some of the tension left her at this

more neutral subject, looking gratefully at Nick, knowing by the compassion she could see in his deep blue eyes that he understood she would rather not talk about Adam. She had brought David here to dinner one evening, had found him the exact buffer she needed to help her get through an evening with Liz, and the other couple had liked him immensely.

'You see rather a lot of him, don't you,' Liz said conversationally.

Leonie at once stiffened resentfully. 'I work for him,' she reminded abruptly.

'I meant socially, silly,' her sister chided.

She looked at Liz with suspicion. What was Liz up to now, trying to absolve her conscience by making sure Leonie had a man in her life when she went to Adam? She was over her own shock and humiliation, needing no man in her life, it was Nick who was going to be devastated.

'I see him occasionally,' she dismissed. 'Very occasionally. Do you see anything of Adam?' she challenged.

Was it her imagination or did Liz suddenly become very engrossed in feeding Emma?

'Occasionally,' Liz replied distractedly, seeing to the baby.

'He came to dinner last week, as it happens,' Nick put in lightly. 'Strange, he didn't mention that he intended seeing you.'

'He meant it to be a surprise,' her voice was sharp. 'And it was definitely that.'

'It must have been,' Liz nodded.

Her mouth firmed. 'I really do have to be going,' she told them determinedly. 'I'll see you again next week.'

It was Nick who walked her to the door, Liz still busy with Emma. Leonie was just relieved at

being able to leave, dreaded these duty visits,
sure that both she and Liz were aware of the
reason they could no longer get on even on a
polite social level.

Somehow knowing she was to see Adam first
thing Monday morning made the weekend pass
all too quickly. But at least he didn't pay her any
surprise visits during those two days; she had half
expected that he would, had felt a sense of anti-
climax when he didn't.

Her hand was a lot better by Monday morning,
the red line of infection having faded up her arm,
the wound feeling more comfortable, so much so
that she felt able to leave off the sling she had
been instructed to wear over the weekend.

'Damn, who can that be?' she muttered as the
doorbell rang as she was brushing her teeth,
grabbing up her silky robe to pull it on over her
lacy bra and panties.

Adam eyed her mockingly. 'Either that's
toothpaste, or you're foaming at the mouth.'

Colour flooded her cheeks as she belatedly
remembered to remove the toothpaste from her
mouth with the towel in her hand. She had just
been so stunned to see him; it was only eight-
thirty in the morning. 'What are you doing here?'
she said ungraciously.

He shrugged, strolling past her into the flat.
'You need a lift to work, I'm here to provide it.'

Leonie followed him in to the lounge, scowling
as Harvey lingered long enough on his way out to
rub against Adam's trouser-covered leg, leaving
ginger hairs on the dark brown material. 'I can
drive myself to work,' she snapped.

He frowned as she freely used her right hand to
prove her point. 'You're supposed to rest that.'

'I did. I have,' she added impatiently. 'It's

better now. Or perhaps you don't take my word for it and would like to inspect it yourself?' she challenged.

'I can see from here that it's in working order again,' he said dryly, making himself comfortable in one of her armchairs. 'Did you have a good weekend?'

'Did you?' she returned.

'Very good,' he nodded. 'Did you visit Liz?'

Her mouth tightened. 'Yes.'

'How is she?'

'Don't you know?'

'If I did, would I be asking?' he reasoned mildly.

'Probably,' she scorned. 'After all, you have to keep up appearances. It's Nick I feel sorry for, he just has no idea does he?' she added disgustedly.

'Leonie, you don't know what you're talking about, so just drop it, hm,' he was still pleasantly polite.

'I know you were having an affair with my sister when we were married——'

'You know I went to bed with her, it isn't the same thing.' Steel had entered his voice.

She gave a disbelieving laugh. 'Of course it's the same thing!'

'No,' he shook his head, his eyes narrowed. 'And one day you're going to want to hear the truth. In the meantime I'd like to concentrate on our affair.'

'I——'

'What did you have for breakfast this morning?'

The question took her by surprise. 'Toast and coffee,' she answered automatically.

'Dry toast and black coffee?' he guessed, standing up. 'The more sophisticated hair-style is an improvement, Leonie, but the loss of weight isn't,' he told her as he went through to the kitchen.

Leonie followed him. 'What do you think you're doing?' she demanded as he took butter, milk and eggs out of the refrigerator.

'Getting our breakfast,' he answered dismissively.

'Haven't you eaten?'

He shook his head. 'I thought I'd wait and eat with you.'

'But I told you, I've already eaten.'

'Rubbish,' he decided, beating the milk into the eggs. 'Go and finish dressing and then come and eat.'

'Adam——'

His gaze was steady. 'I prefer you as you were before you dieted.'

'So you intend fattening me up,' she protested.

'That's the idea,' he nodded. 'I should hurry and dress, Leonie, the eggs will be ready in a few minutes.'

'I'll be late for work!'

'I'm your first appointment, and I don't mind if you're late,' he dismissed with a smile. 'Now off you go,' he gave her bottom a playful tap.

Leonie gave him an indignant glare before leaving the room. How dare he ignore her all weekend and then calmly turn up here again this morning and attempt to take over her life once again!

Her movements quieted as she wondered whether she were more angry at being ignored the last two days or at the fact that Adam was taking command of her life. The answer made her wince.

'Very nice. Very professional,' Adam compli-

mented when she rejoined him in the kitchen.
'Now take off the jacket and put it over that chair
with mine; I'd like to eat breakfast with a lover,
not a businesswoman.'

He had effectively robbed her of her line of
defence! She had donned the formal oatmeal-
coloured suit and brown blouse in an effort to
remain distant from the situation he was trying to
create. But he had discarded his own jacket and
waistcoat, looking ruggedly attractive. With her
own jacket removed they looked like any other
couple having breakfast together before leaving
for work.

'That's better.' Adam divided the scrambled
eggs on to two plates, putting them on the table
with the rack of toast and pot of coffee. He
poured a cup of the latter for both of them as he
sat down opposite her, adding milk and sugar to
Leonie's.

'No——'

'You know you love milk and sugar in your
coffee,' he stubbornly added another teaspoonful
of the latter.

'But it doesn't love me,' she grimaced. 'Adam,
I can't eat that,' she protested as he liberally
buttered a slice of toast for her.

'Then I'll feed you,' he told her throatily,
holding the toast temptingly in front of her
mouth.

'Something else lovers do?' she rasped irritably.

'All the time,' he grinned.

The toast looked so delicious after the strict
diet she had kept herself on the last few months.
She closed her eyes so as not to be tempted,
although the smell tormented her. 'I've only just
given away all my size fourteen clothes to
charity,' she pleaded raggedly.

'So I'll buy you some new ones,' he dismissed.

Her lids flew open at the arrogant statement. 'You most certainly will not!'

'Independent as well as fiery,' Adam smiled at her. 'Eat, Leonie.' The smile didn't leave his face but his tone was firm.

With an irritated glare in his direction she took a bite out of the slice of toast, savouring every morsel; it seemed so long since she had allowed herself the luxury of butter, only keeping it in the refrigerator for guests. But after tasting the toast oozing with butter it was all too easy to eat the fluffy eggs and drink the sweet syrupy coffee.

She frowned as Adam ate his own eggs. 'Why didn't she provide you with breakfast?' she mocked.

'She?'

'The woman you spent the weekend with.'

'Ah, that she,' he nodded, lifting one of her hands to lace her fingers with his. 'I spent the weekend in business meetings, Leonie,' he told her reproachfully.

'That's a new name for it!' She glared at him as he refused to release her hand.

He smiled his appreciation of her humour. 'Would it bother you if I had spent the weekend with another woman?'

'Would it bother you if I had spent the weekend with another man?'

'Like a knife being twisted inside me,' he answered without hesitation.

Leonie gasped, meeting his steady gaze. 'Did you really spend the weekend working?' she asked uncertainly.

'Yes.'

'Why?'

'So that I had time to spare this week to concentrate on my reluctant lover,' he teased.

'And did you spend the weekend alone?'

'My personal assistant——'

'Ah.'

'Jeremy,' he finished pointedly. 'Accompanied me.'

'I see,' she chewed on her bottom lip. 'I spent the weekend alone too.'

'I know,' he nodded, standing up to clear away the debris from their meal before shrugging back into his waistcoat and jacket.

Leonie glared at him. 'If you're still having me followed——'

'I'm not.' He held out her own jacket for her.

She shoved her arms into the sleeves, turning to frown at him angrily. 'Then how did you know I spent the weekend alone?'

He grinned. 'Harvey told me.'

'Adam!' she warned tightly.

He bundled her out of the door. 'The only man you've been seeing since we separated is David Stevenson, and he mentioned at lunch on Friday that he was going away this weekend.'

'Oh.' She looked at him resentfully as they emerged out into the street, the BMW parked behind her orange, and rusty, VW. The difference in their cars seemed to echo the difference in themselves, Adam a man of caviar and fresh salmon, Leonie fish and chips and McDonalds. 'I'll meet you at your office,' she told him abruptly.

'Leonie?' he probed her sudden withdrawal even from arguing with him, frowning heavily.

'We're already late, Adam,' she sighed wearily. 'And my car isn't the most reliable of machines.' She unlocked the door.

'Is that yours?' excitement tinged Adam's voice as he walked over to the VW, touching one fender almost reverently. 'I used to have one exactly like it. I kept it until it just about disintegrated on me,' he chuckled reminiscently. 'You're lucky to have found one in such good condition.'

'Adam, the car is ten years old! And when did you ever have an old jalopy like this?' she scorned.

'When I was at college. Dad wanted me to buy something more prestigious,' he recalled dryly. 'But I'd worked in a bar in the evenings to buy my VW, I wasn't giving it up for anyone.'

He knew exactly how she felt about this rusty old car! He had given her the Porsche during their marriage, and there could be no doubting that it was a fantastic car, but even though she moaned and groaned about the unreliability of the VW she wouldn't exchange it for the Porsche at any price, had worked hard to buy this car for herself. And Adam knew how she felt. Why couldn't he do something, *anything*, so that she could dislike him once more!

'I'll meet you at your office,' she repeated lightly, climbing into her car.

With a shrug of his broad shoulders Adam strolled back to the BMW, sitting inside the car as he waited for life to spark in her engine. As usual the VW played up, and Leonie was hot with embarrassment by the time the engine roared into life, instantly stalling it and having to start the process all over again.

Mrs Carlson's brows rose questioningly as they entered the top-floor suite together, and Leonie blushed at what the other woman must be thinking about them; she had last seen them going to lunch together on Friday. She felt sure the secretary imagined they had spent the weekend together!

'Mr Spencer is waiting for you in your office,' she informed Adam coolly, obviously disapproving of the relationship between her boss and an employee, albeit an indirect employee.

'Thanks, Stella,' Adam dismissed. 'Could you bring in coffee for three?' he requested arrogantly as he ushered Leonie into his office.

A young man stood up at their entrance, his smile warm and friendly as he looked at Adam, cooling slightly as his gaze passed to Leonie, looking her over critically.

Leonie did some 'looking over' herself! The slightly overlong blond hair was deliberately styled that way, she felt sure, the face too good looking to be called handsome, his body slender, wearing the cream suit and brown shirt well, his hands long and thin, the nails kept short—and manicured.

Adam met her questioning gaze with suppressed humour. 'Leonie, this is Jeremy Spencer, my Personal Assistant,' he introduced softly. 'Jeremy, this is Leonie Grant, the young lady who is going to transform these offices into something approaching comfort.'

Leonie was aware of his amused gaze on them as she and Jeremy continued to eye each other critically.

'Miss Grant,' Jeremy Spencer made no attempt to shake hands with her. 'I hope you won't attempt to change the decor too much, I think this is exactly Adam already.'

She looked around the austere room, knowing that it needed light, that perhaps it would have suited the man she had been married to, but not the Adam she now knew, not the Adam that was her lover. 'It is very—masculine,' she agreed.

Jeremy Spencer turned back to Adam. 'I brought these contracts in for you to sign.'

Leonie was ignored by both men during the next few minutes as they discussed the contract that had obviously been decided upon during the weekend, unable to resist making a comparison between them as they bent over the desk. Jeremy Spencer didn't attract her at all!

He nodded to her abruptly when it came time for him to leave, and Leonie had trouble holding in her laughter until the door had closed behind him. 'Really, Adam,' she finally spluttered with laughter. 'What on earth made you employ *him*?'

Adam shrugged dismissively. 'He's harmless. Now come over here, we haven't had our morning kiss yet,' he invited huskily.

'Were we supposed to have one?' she delayed mockingly.

'But of course.' He strolled over to her, his arms about her waist as he moulded her body to his. 'After a weekend apart we shouldn't be able to keep our hands off each other!'

'Then how have we managed to?' she taunted.

'After the way you greeted me this morning I was afraid to touch you until I'd fed you!'

'You aren't afraid of anything,' she scorned. 'You never have been.'

'I'm afraid that if you don't kiss me I'm going to burn up with wanting you,' he groaned.

Her breath caught in her throat, her head tilted back to receive his kiss, her lips parting beneath his, her arms moving about his waist beneath his jacket. He felt warm and solid, his smooth jaw smelling faintly of limes.

'Adam, I forgot—Oh.' An astounded Jeremy Spencer stood in the doorway, staring at them in disbelief.

'Yes, Jeremy, what is it?' Adam's voice was

terse as he kept Leonie in his arms, the evidence of his arousal pressed against her.

'I—er—I forgot to get your signature on these letters.' Jeremy ignored Leonie as he placed the letters on the desk for Adam. 'I had no idea I was interrupting—something,' he added.

Adam eyed him warningly. 'Nothing that can't be continued after you've gone,' he dismissed. 'I'll sign the letters later,' he drawled as the younger man made a hasty departure.

'You've shocked him,' Leonie reproved.

Adam scowled. 'That's nothing to what he just did to me!'

She laughed softly at his obvious discomfort. 'You'll get over it.'

'Maybe—for a while,' he added warningly. 'But it will only be a delay, Leonie, not a reprieve.'

She blushed at the promise behind the words. 'Isn't it time we got down to business, I do have other clients besides you, you know.'

'None that can't wait,' he announced raggedly. 'I have no intention of discussing anything until I've received a proper good-morning kiss, with a certain amount of feeling.'

'That's blackmail,' she protested.

Adam grinned. 'Terrible, isn't it?' He didn't sound in the least repentant.

'Both lovers have the same physical power,' she warned as she moved into his arms, she the one to initiate the kiss this time, moving her mouth erotically against his, feeling the accelerated thud of his heart beneath her hand, moving sensuously against him as he groaned low in his throat, squirming away from him as he would have caressed her breasts. 'Good morning, Adam,' she greeted throatily.

He let out a ragged breath. 'That was with a "certain amount of feeling" all right,' he said ruefully.

She smiled. 'I thought so.'

His eyes narrowed. 'Enjoyed it, did you?'

She was well aware of how aroused he was. 'Immensely,' she nodded.

'Hm,' he muttered. 'Let's get down to the business of choosing the decor for this office.'

Leonie worked happily at his side for the remainder of the morning, a satisfied smile to her lips for the whole of the hour it took him to put his desire from his mind—and body; meeting his scowls with a bright smile.

The decisions made about colours and fabrics she had to get back to her office and begin the ordering and arranging, the part Leonie liked the best—apart from the finished result, of course.

'Lunch, I think,' Adam stood up decisively as she packed away her sample books.

She frowned. 'I hope I haven't delayed you.' It was after one o'clock.

'I meant lunch for both of us,' he pulled on his jacket. 'Together,' he added pointedly.

'Oh I don't usually bother with lunch——'

'I'm fattening you up, remember.' He closed her briefcase and picked it up, taking hold of her arm with the other hand.

'I'm still full up from breakfast,' she protested as he marched her out to the lift, blushing as she realised Mrs Carlson had heard her protest. 'Now she must have completely the wrong idea about us,' she muttered crossly as they went downstairs.

'The right idea,' he corrected with a smile.

'My car,' she protested as he led her to the BMW.

'You can come back for it.'

'I haven't forgotten what happened the last time I intended doing that,' she glowered at him.

His only answer was a mocking smile. Leonie seethed all the way to the restaurant, resentful of his high-handedness, feeling as if all decisions were taken from her whenever she was in his company. She had found her independence the last eight months, she didn't need him taking over her life a second time. He——

'Come on, dreamer,' he chided, the car parked, Adam having opened the car door for her and now waiting for her to join him.

She got out resentfully. 'I wasn't dreaming, I—Adam, this isn't a restaurant.' She looked up at the tall building that was almost a national monument.

'No, it's a hotel,' he acknowledged, guiding her into the plush foyer.

'But they won't serve us here,' she whispered fiercely.

'Of course they will,' he dismissed.

'No——'

'Have you ever heard of room-service?' he taunted as he led the way over to the reception.

'Room——? Adam!' She came to a shocked halt.

He turned to look down at her with mocking eyes. 'I've booked us a room for the afternoon,' he announced calmly.

CHAPTER SIX

'You'vE done *what*?' she gasped disbelievingly, staring up at him in horror-struck fascination.

'I've booked us into this hotel for the afternoon,' he repeated softly.

Leonie looked about them self-consciously, sure that everyone must know they were here for an afternoon of illicit sex; no one appeared to be taking any undue notice of them. 'Adam, you can't be serious,' she muttered.

'I am. Very.'

'But I—We—I thought only married people sneaked off to hotels for the afternoon!'

'We are married.'

'I mean people who aren't married to *each other*,' she glared up at him frustratedly. 'Surely you have your apartment for this type of thing?'

'I don't know what you mean by "this type of thing",' he said softly. 'But I have my apartment to live in,' he corrected reprovingly.

'But you took me there last time,' she said desperately as she noticed one of the receptionists eyeing them curiously, sure they must look very conspicuous as she argued with Adam.

'But isn't this more exciting?' he teased.

It was exciting, there was no denying that. She felt deliciously wicked, could feel the heat in her veins at the thought of spending the afternoon in bed with Adam. But they couldn't just disappear for the afternoon, they both had responsibilities. 'Adam, I have to get back to work, and so do you,' she protested.

He shook his head. 'I told you, I intend concentrating on my reluctant lover; I cancelled all my appointments for this afternoon so that I could spend the time with you. I also told Stevenson I would need you all day. He agreed.'

'Oh, Adam, you didn't,' she groaned, sure David would be curious as to why Adam should need her for the whole day when they were only discussing colour and fabrics.

'It's the truth,' Adam told her huskily. 'And that need is getting out of control,' he added pointedly.

Heat coloured her cheeks at his verbal seduction of the senses. 'I feel embarrassed even being here,' she muttered self-consciously.

'Come on, Mrs Smith,' he chuckled as he took her hand firmly in his and strode the short distance to the desk. 'Or would you prefer to be Mrs Brown?' he paused with his pen over the registration card.

'I'd rather leave,' she groaned uncomfortably.

He shook his head, filling in the form before handing it to the waiting receptionist.

'Good afternoon, Mr Faulkner,' the beautiful young receptionist greeted after glancing at the card. 'The "Bridal Suite" has been prepared as per your instructions,' she continued warmly. 'And if you should need anything else please don't hesitate to call.' She held out a key to him.

'I won't,' he nodded curtly, taking the key, not glancing at Leonie as she would have pulled away at the other woman's mention of the Bridal Suite.

'Do you have any luggage?' the receptionist asked as they turned away.

'It's following on later,' Adam told her smoothly. 'A mix-up at the airport.'

'Oh, how annoying for you,' the young woman sympathised.

'Very,' Adam smiled. 'Come along, darling,' he urged Leonie as she stood numbly at his side. 'I know you would like to lie down after the exhausting day we've had.'

'Adam, how could you?' she demanded as soon as the lift doors closed smoothly behind them, breaking out of the numbed surprise that had possessed her. She couldn't believe this was happening to her!

'With a telephone call,' he deliberately mis-understood her.

'I meant how could you pretend to that woman that we've just got married,' she accused. 'What are you going to tell her when our luggage doesn't arrive and we leave in a few hours?'

Adam unlocked the door marked Bridal Suite, pushing the door open for her to enter. 'I could always tell her you left me,' he said softly.

Leonie was too engrossed in the beauty of the suite to detect the rasping edge of truth to his words. Vases of flowers filled every available surface, the olde-worlde decor adding to the feeling of this all being a dream.

'Oh, Adam, it's beautiful,' she told him breathlessly.

'You haven't seen the best part yet,' he assured her, pulling her towards the bedroom.

'Adam, I know what a bedroom looks like,' she blushed at his eagerness to occupy the wide double bed.

'Not just the bedroom,' he mocked, throwing open the adjoining door.

The room was as big as the lounge in the flat, two walls completely covered in mirrors, a huge sunken bath dominating the room. But it wasn't that that held her attention. 'Cham-pagne,' she was already intoxicated without it! 'Isn't that a little decadent in a bathroom, Adam?' she teased.

'Very,' he confirmed with satisfaction, bending down to turn on the water to the bath.

'Champagne next to the bath is hardly in keeping with the modesty of a newly married couple,' she said dryly, wondering what the hotel management had thought of these 'instructions' of Adam's. 'I—Oh, Adam,' her cry of surprise was a mixture of despair and choked emotion. 'It's a jacuzzi.' She watched as the depth of the water foamed and whirled at the flick of a switch.

Adam sat back on his haunches to watch her reaction. 'I think I must have telephoned almost every hotel in London trying to find a Bridal Suite that had a jacuzzi; most of them thought the "sweet young things" wouldn't have progressed to sharing a bath just yet!'

'A telephone call' he had said was all it took to arrange this magical afternoon, and yet he had now revealed it had taken a lot of planning, planning she was sure he hadn't consigned to the easily shockable Mrs Carlson. 'Why, Adam?' her voice was a husky rasp.

'Well I suppose they thought the bride and groom would be a little shy with each other to start with——'

'Not that, Adam,' she spoke quietly. 'Why have you done all this?' She hadn't realised at first, had been too fascinated by the idea of an afternoon in bed with Adam to notice the similarities to their failure of a honeymoon. Admittedly they hadn't stayed in a hotel then, but Adam's house in the Bahamas had also been filled with flowers at their arrival, a bottle of champagne cooling in the bedroom, a jacuzzi in the adjoining bathroom.

That night she *had* been embarrassed at the idea of sharing a bath with Adam, her inhibitions making her shy about revealing her body to him so blatantly. Adam didn't have an inhibited bone in his body, had walked about naked almost from the time of their arrival, teasing her when she wouldn't join him in nude bathing on their private beach.

'We have a few ghosts to put to rest.' Adam stood up as he saw the painful memories flickering in the bottle-green depths of her eyes.

'Not this way.' She shook her head, the memories too vivid to be denied.

'Exactly this way,' he nodded firmly, taking her in his arms. 'I should never have married you,' he murmured. 'Another man may have been more understanding about your shy inexperience, may have given you the confidence in yourself as a woman that I never could.'

She turned away. 'It wouldn't have made any difference,' she reminded gruffly.

'Sex isn't everything between a man and woman.'

'On their honeymoon it is!' she scorned.

He sighed. 'We're here to put those memories to rest, Leonie. Won't you let me try?'

She shook her head tearfully. 'I can't be seduced into forgetting that—that fiasco with champagne and a—a damned jacuzzi,' she told him sharply.

'I admit it would have been better if we could have returned to the villa, but I had enough difficulty getting you here without arousing your suspicions; the Bahamas would have been impossible!'

'Why should you want to try, Adam?' she sighed wearily.

'I want to replace the bad memories with good ones, erase the bitterness of the past——'

'And can you also erase your affair with Liz?' she scorned.

'There was no affair——'

'Your sleeping together, then,' she amended impatiently.

'No, I can't erase that,' he acknowledged heavily. 'But I would like to explain it one day, when you're prepared to listen. Not today,' he refused as she would have spoken. 'We'll erase one memory at a time, and today we're starting with our honeymoon.'

'I want to leave,' she said stubbornly.

'Without testing the jacuzzi first?' he teased.

'Without testing anything,' she looked at him coldly.

He shook his head. 'I can't let you do that.'

'You can't stop me,' she derided.

'And what's that starry-eyed receptionist going to think when you walk out after fifteen minutes?'

'That I did leave you,' she bit out. 'A year too late. If I'd had any sense at all I would have walked out after the honeymoon.'

'This is the honeymoon of our affair,' he told her huskily, not releasing her.

'Affairs don't have honeymoons,' she scoffed.

'This one does,' he insisted. 'It also has a ring.' He took a brown ring-box from his jacket pocket.

'A Woolworth's special, to convince the gullible?' she scorned.

'A Cartier special,' he drawled, flicking open the lid to the box, revealing a flat gold band studded with diamonds.

Leonie gasped at its delicate beauty. 'I can't take that, Adam,' she shook her head.

'Of course you can.' He lifted her resisting left

hand. 'I noticed you no longer wear the rings I bought you,' he pushed the diamond ring on to her third finger. 'I want you to wear this instead.'

She swallowed hard, the ring looking even more delicately beautiful on her slender hand. 'Why?' she choked.

'It's an Eternity ring,' he told her softly.

'Affairs are usually short-term, Adam,' she shook her head.

'Not this one,' he said with a return of arrogance. 'I want you to move in with me, stay with me.'

'We're getting a divorce, Adam,' she reminded exasperatedly.

'After the divorce then, if you think that living together might make that difficult. I think I can wait that long, if I can see you every night at my apartment or yours.'

'Adam, living together would be like being married!' she protested.

'It would be nothing like it,' his voice was harsh. 'You hated being married, remember?'

'Yes,' she shuddered at the memory of how much pain it had caused her. 'I did hate it,' she confirmed vehemently.

He nodded. 'But you've enjoyed the last few days we've been together, haven't you?'

She would be lying if she said she hadn't; it had been the first time she had felt really alive since she left him. 'Yes . . .' she answered guardedly, knowing she was walking into a trap.

'Then wouldn't you like it to continue?'

'It couldn't,' she shook her head. 'Not indefinitely.'

'We could try,' he insisted.

'Adam, you and Liz——'

'I'm sick of feeling guilty about Liz and I!' His mouth was tight.

'But what would happen to us when she finally finds the courage to leave Nick?'

'Leave Nick?' Adam looked astounded. 'She isn't going to leave Nick!'

'Never?' Leonie frowned.

'Never,' he repeated firmly.

'But I thought——'

'I don't care what you thought,' he bit out. 'Liz is one of those women who make their marriage vows for a lifetime!'

Leonie looked at him sharply, wondering if she had imagined the rebuke behind the words; Adam's bland expression seemed to say she had. 'So I'll do as second-best, hm?' she said bitterly.

'You aren't second-best.' His voice was harsh. 'You never were, you never will be. What happened between Liz and I was already over when I met you. God, I've already admitted I should never have married you, but that doesn't mean we can't be together now. The other night was incredible, you can't deny that!'

'No . . .'

'And can you deny that you want me now?'

She knew she couldn't, knew he must be as aware of the pounding of her heart as she was. She did want him, the non-committal affair he was offering very enticing.

'Come on.' Adam sensed her weakening and took advantage of it, beginning to unbutton her blouse. 'Or the bath will be cold and the champagne flat,' he drawled as he slipped the blouse down her arms and moved to the fastening of her skirt. 'And we wouldn't enjoy it then—the way I intend us to enjoy it,' he added with relish as he stripped her naked.

Colour flooded her cheeks as reflections of herself appeared all over the room, looking very pale next to Adam's dark colouring and the dark suit he still wore. 'Are you sure this is a Bridal Suite?' she asked irritably.

'Yes,' he laughed softly. 'But I think it's for the more—experienced, bride and groom.'

'Shouldn't you undress too?' she suggested awkwardly.

'Yes.' He looked at her pointedly.

She had had little experience with undressing men, never taking such an initiative during their marriage, their undressing the other night having taken place in a darkened apartment, not broad daylight, with images of them reflected everywhere! Her fingers fumbled a little at first, but her confidence grew as she saw the effect she was having on Adam, her hand trustingly in his as they stepped down into the water together.

It was such a big bath that they could quite easily have sat facing each other, but Adam had other ideas, sitting down to pull her in front of him, pulling her back to lean against his chest, his arms around her waist.

He nuzzled against her throat. 'We forgot the champagne,' he muttered, the ice-bucket and glasses out of their reach.

'It isn't important.' She already felt intoxicated just from his touch, gasping as his hands moved up to cup the fullness of her breasts. 'Oh, Adam, I——'

'No, don't move,' he instructed as she would have turned in his arms. 'I haven't washed you yet.' He took the soap in his hand and began to lather her body.

By the time they had finished washing each other the bath was filled with bubbles, all inhibitions gone as they frolicked in the water, Leonie facing him now, leaning against his chest as she lay between his legs. 'Do you think we would drown if we made love in here?' The idea had been tantalising her the last few minutes, knowing Adam was as aroused as she was.

'It's too late even if we do,' he groaned as his mouth claimed hers.

They didn't drown, but the carpet around the bath did seem very wet when they stepped out on to it, not bothering to dress but wrapping towels around themselves as they carried the champagne through to the bedroom.

Adam dipped a finger in his champagne to trail it between the deep vee of her breasts.

'Oh, Adam . . .!' she groaned as he licked the wine from her heated flesh, turning in his arms, gasping her dismay as *all* the champagne from her glass tipped over Adam's stomach, dripping down on to the bed. 'Oh no,' she groaned. 'And I was doing so well too!'

'You were,' he agreed seductively.

She blushed. 'No, I meant——'

'I know what you meant,' he chuckled, making no effort to mop up the champagne with the towel he still had draped about his hips. 'Care to reciprocate?' he invited. 'Your clumsiness may be to my advantage this time.'

She knew what he meant, eagerly drinking the champagne from his body, tasting Adam at the same time, feeling the rush of need that engulfed them both as she removed his towel.

'We really should do something about ordering lunch,' Adam mumbled contentedly a long time later. 'I need to keep up my stamina if you're going to keep attacking me in this shameless way.'

'If I'm going to——!' She turned to look at him indignantly, only to find him watching her with one sleepy eye, his mouth quirke[...] amusement. She relaxed. 'Of course, if your [...] is going to slow you down,' she began moc[...] ingly. 'Maybe I should find myself a young[...] lover.'

There was a deep threatening rumble in his chest as he rolled over to trap her beneath him. 'Maybe *I* should just smack your bottom for you,' he growled. 'My age hasn't slowed me down so far, and—Leonie, did you mean what you just said?' he suddenly asked sharply.

She frowned at his sudden change of mood from lighthearted bantering to serious intensity. 'What did I just say?'

'That I'm your lover.'

She blushed. 'Well you are, aren't you?'

'You didn't seem to think so this morning.'

She shrugged. 'That was this morning.'

'And now?'

'We're in bed together,' she stated the obvious.

'And am I your lover?' he persisted, his hand cupping one side of her face preventing her turning away from him.

'Adam, what we just shared was very pleas- ant——'

'It was toe-curling,' he corrected emphatically.

'For you too?' she asked shyly. In her inexperience it had been very special to her, but surely to Adam, a man with many affairs behind him, it couldn't have meant the same thing.

'Especially for me.' His thumbtip moved across her slightly swollen lips. 'It was the way I always wanted it to be between us, before a marriage licence and a wedding ring fouled things up.'

She looked down at the eternity ring on her finger. 'I won't make any demands on you,' she told him huskily.

ou never did,' he said grimly. 'Not even
ual ones.'

Her mouth curved teasingly. 'Those weren't
he demands I was promising not to make,' she
drawled.

'Thank God for that!' He returned her smile.

She laughed throatily. 'Now that I've discovered the—delights of being in bed with you I
may never want to get out!'

'Suits me,' he murmured as his mouth claimed
hers again.

It was after four when they ordered lunch,
Leonie groaning at the amount of food Adam had
ordered. 'I'll get fat,' she grimaced.

'I hope so,' he nodded. 'I really meant it when
I said I preferred you more—rounded.'

'You mean I really can start to eat again?'

'Please,' he said fervently.

They fed each other like starry-eyed lovers,
and every time Leonie saw the diamond ring
glitter on her finger she felt a warm glow. She
wasn't altogether sure what the ring symbolised,
they could hardly remain lovers indefinitely, but
somehow the ring made her feel as if she really
were Adam's lover, and not just a chattel that he
took out for display every now and then. Because
that was what being his wife had been like; surely
being his lover had to be better than that. It *was*
better!

'You like the ring?' Adam saw her glowing gaze
on it.

'If it enables me to play the part of Mrs Smith,
I love it!' she smiled across the table at him.

He laughed softly. 'You can play the part of
Mrs Smith any time you want to, it's a two-way
arrangement.'

'You mean if I want to spend another

afternoon like this I can just call you and you'll meet me here?'

'Well, not here,' he smiled. 'We can only play the newly married couple once, but I'll meet you anywhere else that you suggest.'

It sounded like heaven after the misery of their marriage. 'I think I'm going to like this arrangement,' she smiled her anticipation.

'Didn't I tell you that you would?'

'Now don't go and spoil it by saying I told you so,' she reprimanded. 'I love the ring, and I'll wear it proudly, but it gives you no rights over me other than the ones I choose to give you,' she warned.

'Right,' he nodded.

She eyed him suspiciously, never having known him be this agreeable in the past. 'I won't give up my job.'

'No.'

'And I won't move in with you.'

'Why not?' he frowned, although he made no objections.

She shook her head. 'It wouldn't work, Adam. When I lived with you before you swamped me, I became a nervous wreck, terrified of leaving the apartment in the end in case I did something wrong.'

'I didn't know that . . .'

'No,' she flushed. 'We didn't talk a lot in those days.'

'Then we'll make sure we talk now. Do I swamp you now?' he asked slowly, all laughter gone.

'Not while I have my own home to go to whenever I want to. I just couldn't live with you again, Adam.'

'Okay,' he shrugged. 'If that's the way you feel.'

'You—you don't mind?'

'No, because I'll move in with you,' he stated arrogantly.

'That isn't the idea, Adam,' she sighed. 'I knew this wouldn't work out,' she shook her head. 'I think we should just forget the idea, it was a stupid one, anyway.'

'If you want us to maintain separate households, then we will——'

'Oh, thank you, Adam,' she glowed. 'I would prefer it. I don't——'

'—for the time being,' he finished pointedly. 'Leonie, I can't keep going between two households when I reach sixty!' he said exasperatedly as she looked dismayed. 'The strain would probably kill me!'

'Sixty . . .?' she repeated dazedly. 'You expect us to still be together then?'

'Why not? Eternity is a hell of a lot longer than the twenty-one years it's going to take me to reach that age! At least, I hope it is,' he frowned.

'Adam, if you think an affair between us will last that long why did our marriage fail after only a year?' she reasoned. 'After all, I didn't know about Liz until that last day.'

'No, but I did,' he answered grimly. 'Our marriage never really started, Leonie. I rushed you into it, made all the rules and expected you to abide by them the way that my mother did. But that isn't a marriage, Leonie, it's just legalising the sexual act—and even that didn't work between us then.'

'Is that why you married me, for sex?'

'I married you because I wanted to be with you,' he rasped.

'Did you ever love me?' she asked dully.

'What difference does it make,' he dismissed. '
couldn't make you happy.'

It was a bitter irony that they could now make
each other happy, that they were now closer than
they ever had been.

'I loved you,' she told him softly.

'I know,' he acknowledged harshly. 'And I
hurt you. This way is much better, isn't it?'

She supposed it was—Of course it was! She
just couldn't understand how they could make an
affair work when their marriage had failed. Unless
their expectations were lower, their demands less.

She had married Adam expecting forever, had
thought him the man of her dreams, with no
faults or blemishes. Hadn't finding that he
couldn't banish all the problems of life for her,
couldn't reach her physically when she put up a
frightened barrier, made him less of a Knight in
Shining Armour? She had forgotten she was
married to a mere man, that he had needs and
fears too, had thought only of herself when the
marriage began so badly and continued on its
downward slide. Adam wasn't responsible for
what had gone wrong on their honeymoon, just as
he wasn't solely responsible for the end of their
marriage. She had taken his involvement with Liz
as the easy way out, when in fact she should have
realised she was the one he had married, the one
he was trying to share his life with.

Poor Adam, no wonder the idea of marriage
had been soured for him; the woman he had
chosen for his wife just hadn't been woman
enough to try to be his partner in life, to give him
the same considerations he gave her.

But she was that woman now, could look back
on their marriage with perspective, believed
Adam when he said he hadn't slept with Liz after

heir marriage. Yes, she believed him now, when it was too late, when all he wanted was an affair. But if that was all that could work between them then it was what she wanted too, wanted Adam in her life.

'Much better,' she assured him huskily, standing up to take off the towel that was her only clothing. 'Shall we go back to bed and see just how much better,' she invited suggestively.

Adam needed no second invitation, his own towel discarded long before they reached the bedroom.

CHAPTER SEVEN

'No, Adam,' she said firmly.

After two more days together she had gained enough confidence in their relationship to say what she liked and disliked, and the idea of joining Adam's father for dinner that evening she disliked intensely!

'Why not?' came Adam's calm query over the telephone.

'You can ask me that?' she gasped. 'After the way he always treated me?'

'I was as much to blame for that as he was,' Adam reminded. 'I should have made sure he understood how things are between us.'

'And how are they?' she demanded tautly.

'If he wants to continue seeing me,' Adam told her softly, 'he'll accept you.'

Leonie was well aware of Charles Faulkner's love for his only child; she had often felt jealous of the closeness between them in the past. If Adam refused to visit his father because of her it would break the older man's heart.

'Adam, men don't introduce their lovers to their fathers,' she derided.

'This man does.'

She sighed at his stubbornness. 'And what are you going to tell him about us?'

'Nothing.'

'Nothing?' she frowned. 'Adam——'

'It's sufficient that we're together,' he explained arrogantly.

'Adam, I don't want to see your father again,'

she told him the simple truth behind her objection.

'I'm sure he feels the same way,' he sounded amused. 'He certainly sounded surprised when I told him you would be accompanying me.'

'Then why put either of us through what can only be an embarrassing experience?' She put her hand up in acknowledgement of the night security guard as he passed by on his rounds. She was working late tonight, felt as if she were the only person in the building; it felt good to know Mick was about.

'I thought you said you wouldn't stay hidden as a lover,' he reminded softly.

'And I haven't been!' She was angry with him for reminding her of that; the two of them hadn't exactly been keeping a low profile the last few days, Adam calling for her at the office for lunch, a rose, a real one now, continuing to arrive daily. She wasn't trying to hide their relationship, but neither was she willing to hypocritically sit down to dinner with Charles Faulkner; they both knew their dislike was mutual. 'I'm not going to have dinner with your father, Adam,' she repeated emphatically.

'He's expecting us.'

'Then you go on your own,' she snapped. 'You had no right accepting the invitation without first consulting me.'

'You would have said no,' he reasoned.

'Obviously,' she bit out. 'Now could we end this pointless conversation, I have work to do.'

'It's after seven,' he pointed out.

'And thanks to an insatiable man I know that kept me awake most of the night I didn't get to work until after ten this morning,' she reminded dryly, smiling at Mick as he passed by her open office door on his way back downstairs.

'Are you complaining?' Adam's voice had lowered sensuously.

'No.' She could still feel the warm glow whenever she remembered their nights together, magical nights when they couldn't get enough of each other, seeming intent on making up for the time they had wasted. 'But I am saying I have to work late tonight. I don't expect to be able to leave much before eight o'clock, and I am certainly not going to feel in the mood to cross swords with your father when I do!'

'I can tell that,' he drawled. 'Okay, I'll call him and change it to tomorrow.'

'Adam——'

'And I won't come to your apartment tonight so that you can get a good night's sleep and won't have to work late tomorrow,' he added huskily.

To say that she felt bereft at the thought of not seeing him tonight would be an understatement, the rest of the evening and night stretched before her like a long black tunnel. But she had a feeling Adam knew exactly how she felt, and she wouldn't give him the satisfaction of knowing how much she would miss him.

'That sounds like a good idea,' she agreed lightly. 'I can also get a few jobs done around the flat that I've neglected the last few days. And I'm sure Harvey would welcome my undivided attention for a few hours.'

'You sound as if you're looking forward to an evening without me.' Adam sounded annoyed.

She smiled to herself. She would spend a miserable evening without him, but it would be worth it to know that he didn't realise that. 'Well we did agree we would have a certain amount of freedom in this relationship, Adam,' she reminded brightly. 'And the idea of putting on an old robe, curling up on the sofa with a good book, sounds like heaven.'

'It sounds awful,' he rasped.

'Only because you don't have an old robe,' she mocked. 'And you never relax enough to read.'

'I prefer other methods of relaxation.'

She could just picture the scowl of his face, almost felt it was worth the night without him to have turned the tables so neatly on him. Almost. But she had become accustomed to curling up against him at night, and she knew she would sleep badly tonight. 'Take a hot bath and read for a while, Adam,' she advised mockingly. 'It's just as relaxing.'

'Like hell it is!' he exploded. 'Is that really what you would compare our lovemaking to, a hot bath and a read?' he demanded angrily.

'I didn't say it was as good,' she was enjoying baiting him. 'Only that it's as relaxing.'

'It's the same thing, damn it,' he snarled.

'Is it?' she asked with feigned vagueness, almost laughing out loud at his indignation. 'Adam, are we having our first lovers' argument?' She instilled disbelief into her voice.

'Yes,' he rasped coldly. 'I'll call you tomorrow.' He rang off abruptly.

Leonie put her own receiver down more slowly, knowing she had won that round, but at what price. She had denied herself a night with Adam, and the mood he was in now she couldn't even be sure he would call tomorrow. But she wouldn't go to him, had given in to him too much in the past to follow that pattern again. She looked at the ring on her finger; a long-lasting affair he had said. And she believed him. One little argument wouldn't spoil what they had now.

But that knowledge didn't cheer her up at all, and she had little enthusiasm for work now, her concentration level down to nil. She packed up after a few minutes, deciding she would be better off coming in early in the morning.

'Had enough for one day?' Mick sympathised as he unlocked the door for her to leave.

'More than enough,' she grimaced at the middle-aged man. 'I'll see you early in the morning,' she told him lightly, knowing he would still be on duty when she got to work at seven-thirty tomorrow. It must be a long boring night for him.

It was a long boring night for her too. Her bath was relaxing, so was Harvey's decision to spend the evening in with her for a change, but the book might as well have been written in Chinese for all she understood it, putting it down after several minutes; her favourite romance author deserved a more avid reader than she could provide this evening.

Had she fallen into the trap so quickly, wanting more from Adam than he wanted to give? There could be no doubting that they came together as equals now, but would marriage make so much difference to their relationship? Their approach to each other was different this time around, would a wedding ring and marriage licence really 'foul up' the relationship, as Adam had claimed it had last time. Couldn't he see that it wasn't those things that had ruined their marriage at all, that it had been their attitudes that were all wrong?

Was she saying she wanted to be married to him again? She knew she had changed since their separation, that she was more self-confident now, had independence in her career if not in her

emotions, felt more able to meet Adam on an
equal footing, both intellectually and emotionally,
and certainly physically. God, how quickly she
had changed her mind about being married to
him, how she wished she didn't have to spend
evenings apart from him like this! Could she
accept just an affair now, when she knew she
wanted so much more?

The insistent ringing of the doorbell woke her up,
and with a bleary-eyed glance at the bedside
clock she saw it was after three o'clock in the
morning. She came instantly awake. She had told
Adam that she was sure her obscene telephone
caller wouldn't come here while she continued to
take his calls, but suddenly she wasn't so sure.
And she was very much alone here.

Should she call the police before answering the
door, or try to find out the identity of her visitor
first? The police certainly wouldn't be very
thrilled with her if it turned out to be a false
alarm. She decided to do the latter, moving
warily to the locked and bolted door, knowing
that if someone were really determined to get in
that they could break the locks with one blow to
the door.

'Who—who is it?' she demanded in a hushed
voice, trembling from head to foot.

'Who the hell do you think it is?' rasped an all-
too-familiar voice.

'Adam!' Her hands shook as she quickly
unlocked the door, almost falling into his arms in
her relief, barely noticing he wore casual denims
and shirt, his jaw in need of a shave. 'Thank God
it's you!' she groaned, her face buried against the
warm column of his throat.

His arms tightened about her convulsively as

she continued to tremble. 'Who did you think—
Oh no,' he groaned, holding her closer. 'You
thought it was him, didn't you?' he realised,
closing the door behind them.

'Yes,' she shuddered.

'I'm sorry, baby. God, I'm sorry,' he muttered
over and over into her hair, holding her until the
trembling stopped and she pulled out of his arms.

'Sorry!' she glared at him. 'You frighten me
half to death and all you can say is you're *sorry!*'
After the relief came her anger, and she was truly
furious!

'I'm *very* sorry?' he said hopefully.

'That doesn't make up at all for the scare you
gave me,' she snapped. 'Just what do you think
you're doing here at three o'clock in the morning
anyway?' she demanded to know.

He sighed, thrusting his hands into the back
pockets of his already tight denims. 'I couldn't
sleep——'

'Well you can take your damned insomnia
somewhere else!' she told him angrily.

'You don't mean that.'

'Oh don't I?' she challenged recklessly. 'You
just turn around and walk out that door. And if
you want to see me again you can call at a
reasonable time!'

'Have you been able to sleep?'

'Of course, why shouldn't I?' In fact it was
because she had only eventually fallen asleep
about an hour ago that was making her so bad-
tempered, feeling nauseous with the suddenness
of her wakening.

'Because you missed me,' he suggested huskily.

'Don't flatter yourself,' she said heatedly. 'I
slept before you came into my life, and I'll sleep
the times you aren't with me!'

His mouth tightened. 'You really want me to leave?'

'Yes!' She glared at him, still badly shaken from her imaginings of him being her obscene caller. 'What we have is a *relationship*, Adam. I'm not some available body you can take to help you fall asleep!'

He recoiled as if she had struck him. 'It wasn't like that——'

'Wasn't it?' she accused. 'Can you deny you came here to make love with me?'

'That was part of it——'

'I'm beginning to think that might be all of it,' she scorned. 'Now that I'm not such a non-event in bed you can't do without it, can you?'

A white line of fury ringed his mouth. 'You have improved in bed,' he bit out contemptuously. 'But I've had better,' he added woundingly. 'I thought this,' he twisted up her left hand with his eternity ring glittering on her finger, 'meant we had more than a physical relationship. I thought we had respect and liking, maybe even loving. But I was obviously wrong,' he thrust her hand away from him. 'I came here because I couldn't sleep until I'd apologised for the senseless argument we had earlier,' he ground out. 'But you obviously haven't been plagued by the same need. I will leave now, I'm sorry I troubled you!'

The colour had come and gone again in her face as they hurled the hurtful words at each other, knowing she had provoked this scene, a scene that could be the end of them. And suddenly the idea of Adam walking out of her life became too unbearable to contemplate.

'Adam!' She ran to him as he stopped at the door, her arms about his waist from behind as she rested her cheek against his back. 'I'm sorry,' she said breathlessly. 'I shouldn't have said those things.'

He didn't move. 'The point is, did you mean them?'

'No,' she sighed. 'I've just woken up after lying awake for hours aching for you,' she admitted gruffly. 'I'm a bad-tempered witch, and I'm sorry.'

The tension left his body in a ragged sigh. 'Can I stay?'

'Please,' she groaned her need.

He turned to take her in his arms, holding her tightly. 'Have you forgiven me for frightening you like that?'

'Of course.' She snuggled up against him.

'Has he called again?'

She shook her head. 'No, I told you, only Fridays at eleven-thirty.'

'I wonder why that is,' Adam frowned.

'Maybe that's his night out with the boys away from his wife,' she dismissed.

'You think he's married?' Adam's frown deepened.

'I try not to think about him at all,' she told him firmly. 'And I wish you wouldn't either. He's a sick man who vents his frustration on life by telling me dirty things.'

'If I ever find out who he is I'll kill him,' Adam ground out.

She smoothed the anger from his face. 'We'll probably never know, so let's forget him.'

'Yes.' He did so with effort. 'Shall we go to bed?'

She smiled up at him encouragingly. 'I thought you would never ask!'

Their lovemaking was different again tonight,

as enjoyable as it always was, but no more so than the closeness they shared afterwards as they lay in each other's arms. As she lay next to Adam Leonie knew that their relationship had transcended the physical, that even though she had no idea of Adam's feelings for her that she loved him, doubted she had ever stopped.

She could feel the tension rising within her as they neared Adam's father's house, wished with each passing minute that she had stuck to her decision not to go there with him for dinner. But her closeness to Adam that morning had compelled her to change her mind, sure at that time that she could survive the ordeal of meeting his father again.

She had changed her mind back again since then, had picked up the telephone a dozen times during the day to tell Adam to cancel the dinner, only to replace it again without speaking to him, sure he would find her cowardly behaviour less than attractive.

Getting herself ready had been a disaster, not realising her nail-polish wasn't dry, finding out that fact when her tights got stuck to it as she tried to get dressed. Then she had torn the hem of her dress with her evening shoe, having to change her make-up tones with the dress, realising at the last minute that she had grey shadow on one lid and green on the other!

By the time Adam arrived to pick her up at seven-thirty she was feeling hot and flustered, telling him she couldn't possibly go out, that she thought she might be going to come down with something. His method of persuasion had left her even more hot and flustered—but with a decided glow to her eyes.

The fact that they were now going to arrive very late didn't seem to bother Adam in the slightest, the intimate smiles he kept directing her way reassuring her that she had his support, that he wouldn't let her down as he had so much in the past.

The Faulkner staff must have been aware of the break-up of Adam's marriage, and yet the haughty butler didn't so much as bat an eyelid at Leonie accompanying Adam to dinner, his manner very correct as he took her jacket.

'Dad doesn't eat little girls for breakfast,' Adam teased her as she hesitated about entering the lounge where she knew the senior Mr Faulkner was waiting for them.

'That's only because he knows I'd give him indigestion!' she muttered ruefully.

Adam was still laughing when they entered the lounge, although Leonie sobered as she sensed the disapproval emanating from the rigid-backed man standing across the room from them. Charles Faulkner was an older version of Adam, still very good looking despite being over seventy, although the lines of harshness beside his nose and mouth weren't quite so noticeable in his son yet. And if Leonie had her way they never would be!

'You're late,' Charles Faulkner bit out critically without greeting.

'Are we?' Adam dismissed unconcernedly.

'You know you are,' his father said harshly, cold grey eyes turning to Leonie. 'What have you been up to now?' he scorned.

In the past she would have cowered away from such open contempt, but somehow tonight she knew Adam was on her side, and that gave her the confidence to steadily meet those critical grey eyes. 'Good evening, Charles,' she deliberately used the informality she had been too nervous to take while living in this house. 'I hope you're well,' she added politely.

The older man scowled. 'I'm as you see me.'

Her perusal of his rigidly held body was deliberate and slow. 'You're looking very well—considering your age.' Her expression remained deceptively innocent, although she could sense Adam was having difficulty containing his amusement.

'And what does age have to do with it?' Charles frowned heavily at the backhanded compliment.

'Well, I remember your once telling me you're just an old man who wants to see his son happily settled before you die,' she reminded him of the argument the two of them had had just before she left Adam; it had been one of many occasions when Charles Faulkner had verbally attacked her without Adam's knowledge. She didn't intend to bring those arguments to Adam's knowledge now, she just wanted to warn Charles Faulkner that she wouldn't stand for it a second time. From the look on the older man's face it was working.

'Oh?' Adam sounded suspicious.

'Don't worry, darling,' she gave him a bright reassuring smile, enjoying Charles Faulkner being the one to feel uncomfortable for a change; in the past she had never dared to mention his father's cruelty to Adam. 'I assured your father I only wanted the same thing.'

Adam looked across at the older man with narrowed eyes. 'It sounds an—interesting conversation.'

'Oh, your father and I had a lot of interesting

conversations,' she dismissed with feigned innocence. 'I've missed them the last few months.'

'I'll bet you have,' Adam sounded angry.

'Shall we go through to dinner?' his father
rasped. 'It's been ready almost an hour.'

'Then it should be nicely cooked, shouldn't it,'
his son dismissed hardly.

'Ruined more like,' his father muttered,
shooting resentful glances at Leonie, which she
promptly ignored.

'I've never known Mrs Simmonds to ruin a
meal,' Adam insisted.

'Always a first time,' his father bit out.

The meal was delicious, as they had all known
it would be. Emily Simmonds was as taciturn as
her employer, but her food melted in the mouth,
and it was always perfectly cooked, the Beef
Wellington, asparagus tips, and tiny new potatoes
that followed the home-made pâté better than
could be bought in any restaurant. But the food
didn't seem to have improved Charles Faulkner's
mood at all.

'You never did tell me why the two of you were
so late arriving,' he snapped as they were served
the chocolate meringue for dessert.

Delicate colour heightened Leonie's cheeks as
she left it to Adam to reply; after all, *he* was the
one who had delayed them. Even if she had
enjoyed it.

'I took Leonie to bed and made love to her,' he
stated calmly, continuing to eat his dessert in the
midst of the furore he had created.

'Adam!' Leonie gasped her dismay, not
expecting him to be quite so candid.

His father's mouth was tight. 'In my day a man
didn't discuss taking his wife to bed.'

'Only other women, hm?' his son mocked, the

elderly man spluttering his indignation. 'But Leonie is no longer my wife.' His hand clasped hers, his smile warm.

'You're back together,' his father pointed out abruptly.

'And we're staying that way,' Adam nodded. 'But not as husband and wife.'

'You—you mean you're just going to *live together*?' Charles made it sound decadent.

'Not even that yet,' his son replied happily. 'Not until Leonie is ready for it.'

'Leonie!' his father snorted. 'In my day a man didn't ask his wife's permission to do anything!'

'I know that,' Adam nodded. 'And for a while I followed your example. I walked all over Leonie as if she were a piece of the furniture, didn't ask her opinion on anything, didn't even care if she wanted to make love or not. I did, and that was good enough for me.'

'Adam . . .!' She looked at him pleadingly.

'No, Leonie, I have to make my father understand that things are different now.' He turned to the older man. 'Leonie is a person, with feelings and desires. It took me a long time to realise there was more to a marriage than putting a ring on some lucky woman's finger. Lucky!' he scorned. 'Leonie never knew a day's happiness after I married her. I was so busy being the strong man you had taught me to be that I killed the love Leonie had for me. I realise now that mother was just as unhappy with you as Leonie was with me.'

His father flushed with rage. 'Your mother wasn't unhappy! I gave her everything, cars, jewels, furs, this beautiful house, the servants, *you*!'

'You didn't give me to mother,' Adam contradicted impatiently. 'You created me together. And instead of giving things to mother you should have spent more time with her, talked, *laughed.*'

'I had a business to run,' his father scowled. 'I didn't have time for that.'

'Then you should have made time!'

The two men glared at each other, the similarity between them at that moment unmistakable.

'And I suppose that's what you intend doing, so that you can pander to this—to this——'

'To Leonie, yes,' Adam bit out.

'And the business will suffer because of it!'

'The business will do just fine,' Adam corrected. 'That's what delegation is all about.'

'I'm surprised you haven't decided to sell everything off,' his father scorned.

'I thought about it——'

'Adam!' Leonie gasped her shocked dismay.

'And decided against it,' he finished gently, squeezing her hand reassuringly. 'There would have been no point,' he shrugged. 'I would still have been the same selfish man, and a richer but unemployed one too. So I decided that it was *I* who had to change, not my life.'

'There's nothing wrong with you,' his father told him tautly. 'At least, nothing that can't be straightened out as soon as you're over this infatuation you suddenly have for your own wife!'

Adam shook his head, his smile sympathetic. 'There's nothing sudden about my feeling for Leonie, I was just too busy to express them before. Never show any sign of weakness, that's your motto, isn't it, Dad?'

'It's never failed me,' the older man ground out.

'Oh it's failed you,' Adam contradicted gently. 'Mother was never completely happy, never really sure of your love, and I've turned out to be made from your own image.'

'There's nothing wrong in that,' his father bit out. 'You're a successful man, well respected in the business world.'

'The respect of complete strangers doesn't mean a lot,' Adam told him impatiently.

'I suppose you're going to tell me next that all you want is Leonie,' his father derided coldly.

'Yes,' Adam answered quietly. 'That's exactly what I want. I also want *your* respect for her, and until you can give her that we won't be coming here again.'

'Adam.' She looked up at him pleadingly.

'It's all right, Leonie,' he assured her with a gentle smile, pulling her to her feet at his side. 'I'm sure my father knows I mean what I say.' The last was added challengingly.

'You're acting like an idiot, Adam,' his father rasped. 'Can't you see she's a little simpleton? Why, all she's been able to do for the last half hour is gasp your name in varying degrees of incredulity!' he added contemptuously.

'Good night, Father,' Adam told him flatly, guiding Leonie to the door.

'Adam!'

He turned slowly at the anguished cry. 'Yes?' he bit out coldly.

His father was standing too now, looking more disturbed than Leonie had ever seen him. 'Can't you see you're making a damned fool of yourself, and over a young slip of a girl who isn't worthy of you?'

Adam gave his father a pitying smile. 'If this is making a fool of myself I hope I never stop!' He opened the door for Leonie to precede him out of the room.

'Adam . . .!'

He ignored his father's second plea, his arm about Leonie's waist as they left the house together.

CHAPTER EIGHT

LEONIE sat quietly at his side as he drove them back to her flat, all of their nights spent there together, Adam an integral part of her life now.

She was stunned by the evening with Charles Faulkner, had had no idea Adam meant to issue his father such a challenge because of her. She knew Adam had changed since their separation, but she hadn't realised just how much.

And he had done it for her, he had revealed tonight, that was what she found so incredible. He wanted her so much that he was willing to change his whole life for her. Surely that must mean he loved her? It was a word that remained conspicuously absent from their relationship.

But she loved him, more than ever after his defence of her in front of his father, knew that she had never really stopped loving him. And she believed him when he said Liz was out of his life for ever. But she wanted to be his wife again more than anything, wanted the children with him even a long-term affair couldn't give them. Maybe in time . . .

'Thank you, Adam,' she huskily broke the silence.

'For what?' He heaved a ragged sigh. 'For subjecting you to even more unpleasantness from my father?'

She put her hand on his thigh. 'I've known worse from him.'

'I'm sure you have,' he ground out. 'Just how often did he used to make those digs at you without my knowledge?'

'It's over now, Adam——'

'How often, Leonie?' he demanded stubbornly.

She sighed. 'Whenever he could,' she admitted. 'It was very demoralising.' She had no intention of widening the gulf between father and son by telling Adam how often his father had reduced her to tears.

'You should have told me what was going on,' he rasped.

Leonie shrugged. 'He never said anything that wasn't the truth. It really doesn't matter now,' she assured him.

'It matters to me,' Adam bit out. 'I was such a lousy husband I couldn't even see what a bastard my father was to you!'

'You were not a lousy husband,' she defended.

'Yes, I was,' he nodded grimly. 'God, I hope I'm a better lover than that!'

She felt any hope she may have had of persuading him to resume their marriage slipping away from her. It was obvious that Adam preferred things the way they were. 'Yes,' she told him softly. 'You're a better lover.'

She fed the cat when they got in, Adam watching her with brooding eyes as he sat on one of the armchairs. He still seemed very disturbed by the incident with his father, and she sat down on the carpeted floor in front of him as she turned to talk to him.

'He'll come around,' she said softly.

He looked startled. 'You mean Dad?' His brow cleared. 'Yes, he'll come around,' he acknowledged heavily. 'And I hope he's a wiser man for it.'

'But you weren't thinking about him, were you?' she probed.

'No,' he admitted flatly. 'I was just wondering

how you could have stayed with me as long as you did, and what damned arrogance made me assume I could just walk back into your life and get you to accept me as your lover!'

'But I did, didn't I?' She smiled up at him.

'Yes, you did.' He shook his head in amazement. 'I thought I had changed after you left me, you see I tried to do exactly that, but now I realise I'm still as arrogant, that I haven't changed in that respect at all. What right do I have to expect you to waste one day of your life on me after what you went through when you were married to me?'

'It isn't wasted,' she assured him huskily.

'And if I hurt you again?' he rasped.

She shook her head. 'You won't.'

'How can you be sure?'

'Why should I want to be?' she cajoled. 'One thing I've learnt from our marriage, Adam, is that the whole of life is a risk. You simply have to live it the way that is best for you.'

He pulled her up to sit on his knees. 'And this is best for us, isn't it, Leonie?' he said fiercely.

'Yes,' she said softly, hope completely gone. 'This is right for us.'

She met his kiss halfway, their emotions spiralling rapidly, standing up in unison to go to her bedroom, needing more than just caresses.

They had barely reached the bedroom when the telephone began to ring, Adam frowning heavily as he glanced down at his watch. 'Friday, eleven-thirty,' he muttered darkly. 'He's consistent, isn't he,' he ground out, turning to pick up the receiver.

'No, Adam, let me——'

He easily shrugged off her attempt to take the receiver from him, listening to the man in silence for several seconds. 'As I said before, it all sounds

very interesting,' he finally cut in gratingly. 'But
if you don't stop these calls I'm going to do some
heavy breathing of my own—down your damned
neck! Do I make myself clear?' He shrugged,
putting down the receiver. 'He hung up.'

'Wouldn't you?' she teased, relieved that the
call was over for another week.

Adam sighed. 'Leonie, he worries me. I know
you say he's harmless, but——'

'He is,' she insisted. 'And maybe now that he
realises I have an aggressive lover he'll stop
calling.'

'Maybe ...' But Adam didn't sound convinced.

'Darling, let's not think about him now,' she
moved sensuously against him. 'Can't you see
this is exactly what he wants?' She sighed as she
received no response. 'Adam, don't let one sick
person ruin everything that we have.'

He looked down at her with pain-darkened
eyes. 'If anything happened to you ...!' His arms
came about her convulsively, carrying her over to
the bed to make love to her until she begged for
his possession, until neither of them had a lucid
thought in their head other than pleasing each
other.

Adam still lay next to her when she woke the
next morning, and with a contented sigh she
realised neither of them had to go to work this
morning. She looked down at the man at her side,
remembering the incredible night they had just
spent together, a night when Adam seemed
determined to possess her time and time again,
and had.

'Adam ...?'

His lids opened instantly she spoke his name,
almost as if her voice were all that were needed to

wake him. A light glowed in his eyes as he saw the sensuality in her face. 'Again, Leonie?' he said huskily.

'Please,' she encouraged throatily.

It was after eleven when they woke the next time, Leonie resisting Adam's caressing as she insisted they needed food rather than more lovemaking. It was while they were eating the brunch Adam had prepared that she remembered she should have visited Liz and Nick that morning.

'What is it?' Adam was sensitive to her every mood, fully dressed as he sat across the table from her, although he had told her he intended bringing some of his clothes here the next time he came, sick of dressing in the same clothes he had worn the evening before. He did look rather out of place in the tailored black trousers and white evening shirt, although he had dispensed with the dinner jacket that completed the suit.

'Nothing,' she dismissed, not wanting to do or say anything that would dispel the harmony of the morning.

'Leonie?' he prompted reprovingly.

She shrugged narrow shoulders, wearing denims and a cream cotton top. 'I should have visited Liz and Nick this morning, but it isn't important. I can call them later.'

'There's still time——'

'I'd rather stay with you,' she said huskily.

'I have an appointment myself at twelve-thirty.' He sipped his coffee.

'Oh?' she frowned, had imagined they would spend the day together.

'Yes.' He didn't enlarge on the subject. 'And I have to go home and change first,' he added ruefully. 'So you can still go to Liz's if you want to.'

It seemed that she might as well when he put it like that. But she couldn't help feeling curious about who he was seeing at twelve-thirty; he wasn't exactly keeping it a secret, but he didn't seem anxious to talk about it either.

'Well, if you're sure,' she frowned.

'I am,' he nodded. 'I'll come back here around six, okay?'

'Okay.'

His sharp gaze narrowed on her. 'What's the matter?'

'Nothing,' she dismissed with a bright smile.

Adam smiled. 'I know you well enough to realise when you're sulking——'

'I do not *sulk*!' she claimed indignantly.

'Yes, you do,' he chuckled. 'Your bottom lip pouts—like that,' he touched the passion-swollen redness with the top of his thumb, 'and your eyes get stormy.' He looked into the glittering green depths. 'Like that. Yes, you're definitely sulking. What is it, Leonie?' he prompted softly.

She shrugged. 'I thought we were going to spend the day together, that's all,' she admitted moodily.

Pleasure glowed in his eyes. 'Tomorrow we won't even get out of bed,' he promised. 'But today we have our courtesy visits to make, you to Liz and Nick's, I to a business meeting.'

'On a Saturday?'

'Sometimes it's the only time that's convenient. But if you would rather I didn't go . . .?'

'Oh no,' she denied instantly, not wanting him to think she was acting shrewish, as he had once claimed a wife's possessiveness could be. 'I'll cook us dinner this evening.' That way they could spend more time alone together.

'It's about time *you* cooked me a meal.' He mocked the fact that he was the one who had once again done the cooking.

'You never used to like my cooking,' she reminded softly.

'That isn't true,' he sobered. 'You used to get yourself in such a state about it if something went wrong that I thought you would prefer to eat with my father. I couldn't have given a damn if some of the food was a bit burnt around the edges!'

'It was usually burnt all over,' she grimaced.

'Didn't you know that I didn't give a damn if it was charcoaled?' he rasped. 'I didn't even notice what I was eating, I was too busy looking at my wife!'

'Oh, Adam,' she choked. 'Tonight I'll cook you something really special,' she promised. 'It's just that I've been too exhausted the rest of the week to be able to crawl from my bed, let alone cook you dinner in the evenings,' she teased lightly.

'Tomorrow you won't have to bother,' he promised, standing up to pull on his jacket.

'I may starve,' she warned.

'You won't.' His gaze held hers before he bent to kiss her.

'Man—or woman—cannot live on love alone,' she told him.

'We can try,' he murmured throatily, shaking his head as he moved away from her. 'If I don't leave now, *I* may not have the strength to get out the door.' He gave her a quick kiss on the lips. 'I'll see you this evening, darling.'

Her flat seemed very empty once he had left, not even Harvey's presence as he jealously followed her from room to room helping to dispel the feeling of loneliness as he usually did. Accustomed to sleeping on the bottom of her bed at night he wasn't too happy about being relegated to the sofa in the lounge this last week.

To Leonie's dismay Nick was out when she arrived for her visit, feeling awkward at being alone with Liz, something she had pointedly avoided since the day she had seen her sister in Adam's arms. But she could hardly leave again just because her brother-in-law was out.

But she didn't know what to talk about to Liz, had felt uncomfortable with her sister since knowing she and Adam had been lovers. Luckily feeding Emma and putting her upstairs for her nap filled the first half an hour, although without the distraction of the baby Leonie felt even more awkward.

'That's a lovely ring.' Liz reached her hand across the kitchen table as they sat in there drinking coffee together, admiring the diamond-studded ring on Leonie's slender hand. 'It's new, isn't it?' she looked up enquiringly.

Leonie put the offending hand out of sight under the table. 'Yes, it's new,' she mumbled, wondering why on earth she hadn't thought to take it off before visiting her sister.

'It looks expensive,' Liz sipped her coffee.

'I—It probably is,' she acknowledged awkwardly.

Her sister's eyes widened. 'It was a gift?'

'Yes,' she admitted reluctantly.

'Well don't be so secretive, Leonie,' Liz laughed reprovingly. 'Who's the man?'

She shrugged. 'No one important.' She instantly felt disloyal for dismissing Adam in that way. 'That isn't true,' she said quietly, her head going back proudly. 'Adam gave me the ring.'

'You're back together?'

She wished she could tell more from her

sister's expression how she felt about the idea, but Liz was giving nothing away, her expression guarded. 'In a way,' she finally answered.

Liz frowned at the evasion. 'What does that mean?'

She moistened suddenly dry lips. 'We're together, but not *back* together if you know what I mean.'

'No, I don't,' Liz looked puzzled.

'Our marriage was a failure, being with Adam now is nothing like that.'

'But you are—together?' Liz persisted.

She drew in a deep breath, not wanting to hurt her sister as Liz had hurt her in the past, their roles somehow reversed now. 'Yes,' she confirmed abruptly.

Liz let out a long sigh of relief. 'You don't know how happy that makes me,' she said shakily.

Leonie frowned. 'Happy?' It was the last thing she had expected her sister to feel about her reconciliation with Adam. 'You realise I know of your involvement with Adam before we were married?'

'Yes,' Liz nodded. 'I always felt that it was partly that involvement that parted you and Adam.'

Partly! It was her sister's involvement with *her* husband that had ended the marriage!

'I'm so glad Adam has at last explained to you what really happened between us,' Liz said happily. 'He has, hasn't he?' she hesitated.

'I know about it,' she acknowledged curtly.

'Adam always said that knowing wouldn't make things any better between you, that you had other problems that couldn't be worked out.'

'Yes.' But they had worked those problems out now! So what was the secret behind Liz's involvement with Adam, how did her sister think Adam could ever condone their actions so that she could forgive them both?

'I couldn't imagine what they were,' Liz frowned. 'And it wasn't my business to ask. I know how kind Adam is, I couldn't think what could be wrong between you, but Adam insisted that knowing the truth about the two of us would serve no purpose, that things were over between you. I'm so glad he was wrong!'

Leonie had no intention of correcting her sister's assumption that Adam had explained everything to her, knowing that Liz was going to reveal it without realising she was doing so.

'Adam so deserves to find happiness, he was so kind to me. When Nick went through what I can only assume to be his mid-life crisis a couple of years back and had an affair with a young girl at his office I felt so—so humiliated, so—so unfeminine, so unattractive, that I just wanted to crawl away and hide.'

Nick's affair? This was getting more complicated than she had imagined! She made a non-committal noise in her throat, encouraging Liz to continue.

'Adam made me feel like a woman again, a beautiful woman,' she recalled emotionally.

'Wasn't going to bed with you a little drastic?' Harshness entered Leonie's voice. 'Offering you a shoulder to cry on might have been just as effective—and less complicated.'

'*I* was the one who instigated our lovemaking,' Liz admitted heavily. 'It could have been any man, I just wanted to prove, to myself, that I was still an attractive woman.'

'If it could have been any man why did you have to choose *Adam!*'

She shrugged. 'Because I knew he was too kind to rebuff me. He knew I couldn't take any more rejection, acted as if it were what he wanted too, but afterwards we both knew it was a mistake. I still wanted Nick, not Adam, and the only way to get Nick back was to fight for him, to show him how important he was to me, not have an affair myself.'

'You obviously won,' Leonie said dully, the involvement she had believed to be an affair not an affair at all. Then why hadn't Adam told her that! Because he didn't care enough about her to explain himself . . .? Somehow his actions now disproved that.

'Yes, although it wasn't easy,' Liz smiled tremulously. 'Knowing Nick had slept with another woman, was perhaps comparing me to her, was a difficult hurdle to cross.'

Leonie didn't need to be told about that torment, she had *lived* it!

'And I knew I could never tell Nick about the night I spent with Adam,' she sighed heavily.

'But he had an affair himself!'

'Yes,' Liz nodded. 'But to be told that I had spitefully slept with another man because he had betrayed me was something I knew he could never accept. Besides, Adam was married to you by this time.'

'All the more reason for the truth to come out, I would have thought!'

'And what was the truth?' Liz reasoned. 'That Adam had loaned me his body for a night so that I might feel a whole woman again? Why ruin five lives just to ease our consciences?' she shook her head.

Because Leonie had a feeling it was that guilty conscience that had ruined her own marriage,

Adam's guilty conscience that he had once gone to bed with her sister. 'You were never in love with Adam?' she probed.

'No,' Liz denied instantly. 'Or he with me. He took one look at my baby sister and fell like a ton of bricks,' she added ruefully. 'I'd always teased him that it would happen that way for him, and he had always scorned the idea. When I came back from my reconciliation holiday with Nick to be told the two of you were getting married I didn't know whether to be ecstatic for your sake or nervous of losing the happiness I had just refound with Nick.'

'*That's* why you were less than enthusiastic by our news.' She had thought it was for completely a different reason!

'Yes,' Liz grimaced. 'I should have known Adam would never break his promise to me. But when I knew I was expecting a baby it somehow seemed important that he reassure me Nick would never find out about that night I had spent with him. Adam assured me no one would hear of it from him.'

And she had walked in on that scene, had misread it completely. Could Liz be right, *had* Adam fallen deeply on love with her the first time they met? And if he had, did he love her still?

'He told me your marriage wasn't working out,' Liz looked sad. 'That he expected you to leave him any day. I couldn't understand it, the two of you had seemed so much in love. But Adam assured me my behaviour with him had done nothing to cause the rift.'

And he had lied. He had risked their happiness for the sake of her sister's! She knew it as surely as if Adam had told her so himself. But he never would. He *was* kind, had never deliberately hurt anyone in his life. Not even her, she realised now. Two years ago she had been too immature, too starry-eyed, to accept and understand what had prompted him to make love to Liz, a new maturity gave her the insight to realise he had been helping a friend cope with her pain. He couldn't have had any idea at the time that he would fall in love with Liz's young sister, that he would want to marry her even though he knew that, like Nick, she couldn't have taken the truth about him and Liz. When she had found out about the two of them she had acted predictably, hadn't cared that what she had thought to be their affair had taken place before their marriage, that Adam had been completely faithful to her since that time. All she had seen were the black and white facts; Adam had slept with her married sister!

But had he really sacrificed their happiness for Liz's sake? Eight months after their separation they were back together, happier than ever.

And suddenly she needed to tell him she understood the past, that she wanted a future with him, a permanent future, with a wedding ring. There would be no more evasions of the truth between them, she wanted to be his wife, and she intended telling him so.

'He was right.' She stood up to kiss her sister warmly on the cheek, seeing Liz's surprise to the first instantaneous show of affection she had given her in a long time. 'We had other, much more serious problems.' Such as not talking to each other about what was bothering them. She intended remedying that straight away!

'I'm so glad you're back together again,' Liz hugged her.

'So am I.' She gave a glowing smile.

'I hope it works out this time. Adam loves you very much, you know.'

Yes, she finally believed that he did. He had been brought up in a household where love was never expressed openly, found it difficult to show love himself as a consequence, even when he knew it was pushing them apart. While they had been separated he had set about changing a lifetime of emotional repression, of sharing his feelings and fears with another person. The despair he had shown last night when they got back from his father's because he thought he had failed was evidence of that.

It also made her question the affair between them now. What was it he had said the first night they had slept together since their separation, that the affair had been her suggestion? He believed it was what *she* wanted!

It was time they sorted out this mess, to tell each other of their true feelings, for the past and for each other. If an affair were really all he wanted then she would accept that, but she had a feeling they were both living a lie. God, she could hardly wait to see him again!

CHAPTER NINE

THE telephone was ringing as she entered the flat, and after falling over an awkwardly reclining Harvey as he lay in front of the doorway, she ran to pick up the receiver, sure it was Adam.

'Leonie?'

Her hand instantly tensed about the green-coloured receiver. 'Yes?' she sounded breathless.

'You sound as if you've just got out of bed.'

'I——'

'Is he still there, Leonie?' that taunting voice interrupted. 'Is your lover still in your bed?'

This couldn't be happening. This was Saturday, he never called on a Saturday!

'Leonie?' The man's voice had sharpened angrily as she remained silent.

'Yes! Yes, I'm still here,' she gasped, realising that something else was different about this call too. He was using her name! He had never done that before either

'Did your lover stay the night, Leonie?' he rasped.

'Look——'

'Is Faulkner still there with you?' he cut in furiously.

Leonie felt numb with shock. Not only did this man know *her* name, he also knew about Adam! She felt an uncomfortable tingling sensation down her neck, as if someone were watching her. How else could this man know so much about her and Adam? God, it made her feel sick—and frightened. It was a long time since she had felt physically threatened by this man's calls, but today was different, *he* was different, not talking about the sick things he would like to do to her as he usually did, sounding menacing as he questioned her.

'I said is he there, Leonie?' he grated again.

'I—er—Yes, he's here,' she invented desperately, suddenly feeling trapped, out of control of her own life.

'Liar!' the man gave an unpleasant laugh. 'He isn't there, is he, Leonie?'

'Of course he is,' she insisted. 'He—He's in the shower.'

'I saw him leave, Leonie.'

'You saw——!' She swallowed hard. 'Where are you?' Her voice rose shrilly.

'Wouldn't you like to know,' he taunted. 'Get rid of him from your life, Leonie. You're mine, do you understand? he growled. 'I stood by while that wimp Stevenson tried his luck with you, but Faulkner is a different matter. Get rid of him, Leonie, you won't like what will happen to him if you don't.'

'Wh-what?'

'I could love you much better than he ever could,' he told her softly.

'What will you do to Adam?' she repeated shrilly.

There was silence on the other end of the telephone, but she knew he was there, knew he hadn't rung off, could sense him there even though he didn't say a word.

'You're in love with him!' The man suddenly exploded.

'No!' she denied desperately. 'I just——'

'Yes, you are, damn you,' he rasped harshly. 'And I can't allow that, Leonie. I would have given you everything, everything,' his voice rose. 'But you weren't interested, were you? Oh no, you chose Stevenson over me, and now you're in love with Faulkner. You shouldn't have done that, Leonie. I'll never allow another man to have you. Never!' He slammed the receiver down with such force it hurt her eardrums.

She couldn't move, daren't move, felt frozen, her breathing constricted, her hunted gaze darting about the room like a cornered animal.

She had told Adam the man never threatened, but he had threatened just now. She had told Adam she didn't know the man, and yet she obviously did for him to know so much about her. But *who*, who could it be? Every man she had ever met came crowding into her mind, a jumble of male faces that suddenly all looked menacing.

And then she dismissed the majority of them as being too ridiculous; she hadn't seen most of them for years. But that still left so many friends, acquaintances. Two men she knew she could exclude from that list, Adam and David. It couldn't be Adam, she knew that without a doubt, and the man had been so scathing about David he couldn't possibly have been talking about himself.

But there was Tony, the boy she had been seeing casually before she met and married Adam so quickly, several friends of Adam's she had come to know, the man in the upper flat, and the man in the lower one, the men she worked with, the men she had worked for. God, the list was endless, and she couldn't begin to guess which one of them could be this sick.

But she did have to get out of the flat, couldn't stay here and just wait for him to arrive on her doorstep. She had to call Adam, that was what she had to do. It was almost three now, he would be coming to see her soon, and she couldn't possibly let him walk into a trap.

She let his telephone ring and ring, but received no reply, becoming more and more agitated as she didn't. Surely he couldn't still be at his business meeting?

She had to get out of here. She could wait for Adam at his apartment, didn't care how long she had to stand outside; she wasn't staying here.

She moved about the flat picking up her bag and jacket, pushing an unsuspecting Harvey, as he lay asleep on her bed, into his travelling basket; she didn't intend returning here, would have the rest of her things, and Moby Dick, moved to Adam's apartment as soon as she could.

She was just giving one last frantic look round to make sure she had switched everything off when the doorbell rang shrilly. Her breath stopped in her throat, and for a moment she couldn't move. Dear God, what was she going to do? What *could* she do!

She thought of pretending she wasn't here, but the sudden trip she made over the coffee-table, dropping an indignantly screeching Harvey, put lie to that idea. She righted Harvey's basket before moving cautiously to the door, pressing her ear against the white-painted wood. She couldn't hear anything—but what had she expected, heavy breathing!

The doorbell rang again. 'Leonie, are you in there?' called a familiar voice. 'I heard a thump, have you hurt yourself?'

Relief flooded through her as she ripped open the door. 'Gary!' she hugged him before quickly pulling him inside. 'Thank God you're here.' She felt like crying at the sight of a friendly face after her imaginings.

'I just thought I'd drop by for a coffee while Joan does her shopping,' he dismissed in a preoccupied voice, frowning at how pale she was. '*Did* you hurt yourself?'

She shook her head. 'Only Harvey's dignity when I dropped him.'

Gary looked down at the cat in the travelling basket. 'Are you going away?'

'Just to Adam's—Adam Faulkner,' she explained with a blush, although Gary must be as aware as the rest of the staff were at Stevenson Interiors that she was seeing Adam. 'You see, I've been having these calls, nasty calls,' she grimaced. 'I think I told you about them once . . .?'

'Yes,' he nodded.

'Well, I was sure he was harmless. But then he called just now, and he never calls on a Saturday, and I——'

'Hey, calm down,' Gary chided, his smile gentle. 'Why don't you sit down, let me make you a cup of coffee, and then you can tell me all about it.'

'No, we can't stay here.' She shook her head frantically. 'You see, when he called just now he was—threatening. I'm sure he's going to come here,' she shivered.

'With me here?' Gary soothed. 'I doubt it.'

He was a dear, but with his five-foot-eight-inch frame she didn't feel confident she could depend on him if it should come to violence with the obscene telephone caller. But she couldn't say that to him without hurting his feelings.

'I really don't think we should stay here, Gary,' she tried to sound calm. 'Look, why don't you come over to Adam's with me, he's sure to be back by the time we get there.'

'He isn't at home?'

'He had to go to a meeting, and he doesn't seem to be back yet.' She was speaking quickly in her agitation. Didn't he realise how dangerous this situation was! 'Please, Gary, we have to go,' she urged desparately.

'I don't think so.'

'But he could be here any minute! He——' her voice trailed off as she watched him walk over to the door, check that it was locked before putting the key into his pocket. 'What are you doing?' she asked—but she had a dreadful feeling she already knew!

He looked at her calmly. 'Stopping you from leaving.'

She swallowed hard. 'Gary, this isn't a time to play games. He could be here soon, and——'

'He's already here.'

She had guessed that as soon as he pocketed the key—and she had actually *let* him in here! Gary was the man who called her every Friday night, who whispered obscene things he wanted to do to her. She couldn't believe this nightmare, had always believed the two of them were friends.

'Why, Gary?' she asked faintly, feeling weak with nausea that it was him that said such disgusting things to her every week, that he had done so for the last six months, while still continuing to be so friendly at work. God, she had even told him about those calls!

'Why do you think?' he scorned, his eyes narrowed unpleasantly.

'I—I don't know.' She watched him warily, but he seemed to be making no move to cross the room to where she stood poised for flight.

'Because I want you, you little fool,' he derided mockingly. 'I always did, from the moment you came in to my office with David that first morning and promptly fell over the waste-paper basket. You made me feel protective, very much the man as I helped you to your feet. You looked so delicate and defenceless, and I wanted to take care of you.' There was a smile to his lips as he recalled the morning they had met. 'That month I worked so closely with you was the most enjoyable four weeks of my life,' he added flatly.

'I enjoyed it too,' she infused enthusiasm into her voice.

His eyes hardened angrily. 'You barely noticed me!' he rasped.

'You were married——'

'Yes,' he acknowledged harshly. 'But so were you.'

'I was separated from my husband.'

'I remember. I was jealous of any man who had had you and not had the sense to hold on to you. I hated your husband,' he stated coldly. 'I wanted you, no other man could have you.'

'No other man did,' she assured him quickly.

'David——'

'We've only ever been friends, nothing more.'

'Faulkner?'

She swallowed hard, paling even more, knowing after what he had just said about her husband that she daren't tell him Adam was the man she was married to. 'Adam and I are friends too,' she dismissed lightly.

'Very good ones from the amount of nights he's spent here with you,' Gary scorned.

'How did you—Have you been watching me?' she asked dully.

'I didn't need to,' he derided. 'Your face when

you came into work every morning this week has
been enough to tell me just *how* friendly you and
Faulkner have become.'

'Gary, you don't understand——'

'Oh, I understand,' he sneered. 'Like all
women you need a man, any man, to make love to
you and tell you how beautiful you are one
hundred per cent of the time!'

'It isn't like that——'

'That's what Joan said when I found out about
the little affair she had been having with a doctor
at the hospital,' he cut in hardly. 'I'd been
working hard, just wanted to sleep when I finally
fell into bed at night, but the bitch couldn't
understand that. Oh no, she had to go and find
herself a lover to give her what I wasn't!'

She had met Gary's wife at the Christmas
dinner, had found the other woman to be shallow
and flirtatious, had been surprised to learn she
was a nurse, the wine she had consumed with the
meal making her silly and giggly, demanding
kisses from all the men in the party, her willowy
beauty making them all willing to comply.

'You could have left her,' she said softly.

'She would take Timmy with her.' He looked
bleak as he spoke of his young son.

'Gary, can't you see that what you—what
you're doing now is wrong?' she pleaded with his
common sense—if he still had any!

'I haven't done anything—yet.'

She shivered in apprehension at the threat
behind that last word. 'You made those calls,' she
reminded.

'Not at first,' he shook his head.

She frowned. 'What do you mean?'

'I didn't make the first couple,' he sneered.
'And I wouldn't have made any of them if you

hadn't started seeing David. You were really upset when you got the first call, remember, told me all about it. But it was David you let comfort you,' he added harshly. 'David who took you in his arms and told you everything would be all right. And for a couple of weeks the calls stopped, didn't they, Leonie?' he derided.

'And then *you* began making them,' she realised dully. She hadn't noticed a change in the voice, had been too disturbed by the first few calls to notice what it even sounded like!

'Yes,' he admitted with satisfaction. 'It felt strange at first, I didn't quite know what to say. But after a while it just came naturally,' he smiled his relish.

As he became more and more emotionally disturbed! It was his mentally disturbed state that made him so unpredictable now. She didn't quite know what to do next, or what *he* was going to do either!

'You always made such a joke about asking me out, Gary,' she tried to smile, although her face felt stiff. 'I didn't realise you were serious.'

'And if you had you would have accepted, hm?' he scoffed at her attempt to placate him.

'I may have done,' she answered sharply.

'You may have done,' he repeated derisively, his gaze mocking. 'Don't lie to me, Leonie.' His eyes hardened to blue pebbles. 'Joan is always lying to me.' His hands clenched into fists at his sides. 'And I don't like it!'

She could see that, swallowing hard at the anger emanating from him. 'I'm sure she loves you, Gary,' she encouraged. 'Every marriage has its problems, I'm sure Joan regrets her lapse with the doctor.'

'She stills see him.'

'Oh.' Leonie chewed on her bottom lip.

'Once a week,' he spoke almost to himself, not seeming to see Leonie at all at that moment. 'She tells me she's working at the hospital that night, but I've checked; she's seeing him.'

'Fridays,' Leonie realised weakly.

'Yes,' he bit out, focusing on her again.

'She can't really care for him, Gary, otherwise she would have left you to go to him,' she pointed out desparately.

'He's married too,' Gary scorned. 'This way they both have the best of both worlds!'

And Gary's jealousy and pain had acted like a sickness, growing, spreading, until he latched his unwanted love on to another woman—who also turned out not to want him.

'For a while I thought about killing both of them,' he continued matter-of-factly. 'But then I met you, and realised I could have the same arrangement Joan has. You should have gone out with me, Leonie, I would have been so good to you. Now all we'll have is this one night together.'

'Wh-what do you mean?'

'Well you know who I am now,' he shrugged.

'You—you're going to leave London?'

He seemed amused by the idea. 'No,' he drawled.

Leonie felt faint as his meaning became clear to her. She couldn't believe this were really happening—it happened on television, in films, *not* in real life!

'Gary, you're making a mistake,' she told him breathlessly. 'I—I'll forget all about this if you—if you'll just leave,' she urged desperately.

He shook his head. 'As soon as I got out the door you would call the police.'

She would too, knew she would have to. Gary was a danger to other people as well as to himself. But by the sound of it she wasn't going to get the chance to call anyone.

'It would be your word against mine,' she reasoned.

'And Faulkner's,' he grated. 'It was him who answered the last two calls, wasn't it?'

She flushed her guilt. 'Gary——'

'We've talked enough,' he snarled. 'I didn't come here to talk!'

She knew exactly what he had come here for, and the thought of it terrified her. 'Gary, can't you see this is wrong?' she pleaded. 'Do you really want to make love to a woman who doesn't love you?'

'Why not?' he scorned. 'That's what I do at home!'

'But that's Joan, Gary,' she said softly. 'Things could be different between us. We——'

'Don't try the psychological approach, Leonie,' he scoffed. 'I've seen those bad films too!'

'I've always liked you, Gary,' she insisted.

'Then you're going to get the chance to prove it, aren't you?' he taunted. 'And for God's sake shut that cat up!' he rasped as Harvey scratched frantically at the basket to be let out.

Leonie weighed up the possibility of winning a fight against Gary, instantly knowing that she wouldn't, not even with desperation on her side. Gary may be short and stocky, but muscles bulged in his arms and legs. He could overpower her in a few minutes, possibly sooner.

She moistened dry lips. 'If I let him outside he'll stop,' she suggested desperately. 'He—He's likely to keep scratching if I leave him in the basket.'

Gary's mouth twisted. 'By all means throw th
damned cat out. But don't try and scream,' he
warned gratingly. 'You wouldn't like the way I
silenced you,' he promised.

Leonie had a feeling *he* would enjoy it
immensely, her hands shaking as she carried the
wicker basket over to the window, all the time
measuring the distance between herself and
Gary, a plan formulating in her mind. He was too
close, although as Harvey clambered thankfully
out of the window the empty basket in her hand
gave her an idea.

'Hey, Gary,' she called, at the same time
launching the basket at him, knocking him
momentarily off-balance, his language voluble as
she climbed outside on to the ledge that Harvey
used to get to the neighbouring buildings.

Only it wasn't as easy for her to balance there
as it was for Harvey, the nine-inch-wide ledge
that seemed more than adequate for his wiry
frame suddenly seeming too narrow for her to
negotiate with any degree of safety.

'What the hell do you think you're doing?'
Gary's furious face appeared at the open window,
his hand reaching out to clasp her ankle.

She had seen the move coming and scuttled a
short distance along the ledge, sighing her relief
as she realised she was out of his reach, leaning
back against the rough brickwork of the wall
behind her as she swayed giddily, the ground
seeming a very long way down.

'You stupid bitch,' Gary's face was contorted
with fury. 'Get back in here.'

'Are you joking?' she gave a shaky laugh, her
eyes still closed as she fought back feelings of
faintness. 'You *have* to be joking, Gary!'

'You'll fall and break your damned neck!'

She turned to look at him, breathing heavily in her anger. 'Surprisingly enough,' sarcasm sharpened her voice, 'I would find that infinitely more preferable to being attacked by you. Isn't that strange!' she bit out contemptuously.

Some of the bravado left him as he realised she was serious, taking on the look of a man who just didn't know what to do next. 'Leonie, please come back in here,' he encouraged softly.

'No!'

'I promise not to touch you, damn it!'

'You think I believe you?' she derided harshly. 'I wouldn't trust you—Oh!' she gasped as dizziness washed over her once again.

'Are you all right?' Gary sounded desperate. 'Leonie, for God's sake get back in here.'

'I can't,' she shook her head, pushing into the wall behind her, biting her lip as she became afraid to look anywhere but straight ahead.

'I won't hurt you,' he promised vehemently.

'Don't you understand,' she grated between clenched teeth. 'I can't move!'

'What is it? Is your foot stuck somewhere? Maybe if I——'

'No!' she cried her panic as she heard him attempting to climb out on to the ledge. 'Don't come near me,' she warned desperately.

'But if you're stuck——'

'I'm not,' she shuddered. 'I—I have vertigo!' Two floors up, and she was terrified! Heights had never bothered her before, although she did have to concede that the circumstance of her being out here on a nine-inch ledge may have contributed to the fact that she now couldn't move back into the window and couldn't attempt to reach the neighbouring building either! The thought of moving at all terrified her, frozen to the spot.

'The let me help you——'

'Don't come near me,' she warned as Gary would have joined her out on the ledge. 'If you come out here I—I swear I'll jump!'

'But you can't stay there!'

'Why can't I?' she was near to hysteria.

'Leonie, you have to come in some time,' he encouraged.

'And face a raving sex-maniac?' she shook her head vehemently. 'No, thank you!'

'It was only a game——'

'Remember, Gary,' she bit out grimly, 'I watched the same bad films.'

'You would rather stay out there, possibly fall, than come back in here with me?' he sounded exasperated.

'In one word, *yes!*'

'You stupid——'

'Bitch,' she finished curtly. 'I've noticed that seems to be your favourite word for a woman who won't do things your way,' she scorned. 'No wonder Joan found herself another man!'

'You know nothing of my marriage to Joan,' he snarled.

'I know that the failure of it has involved me,' she bit out. 'And I——' she broke off as the telephone in her flat began to ring. 'It's Adam,' she breathed. 'It has to be Adam. If I don't answer that Gary, he'll know there's something wrong.'

'Why should he?' he dismissed logically. 'He'll just think you're still out.'

He was right, of course, but she had to try. 'No,' she insisted. 'He said he would call me. If I—if I don't answer he'll think something has happened to me.'

'Then come in and answer it,' Gary invited softly.

God, the phone would stop ringing in a minute, with the caller—*possibly* Adam, thinking she just wasn't at home!

'I didn't think you would,' Gary said smugly.

'You—you're insane!' She told him angrily as the telephone stopped ringing, the silence it left unnerving.

'I thought you had already concluded that,' he dismissed. 'I'll be waiting inside if you should change your mind about coming in,' he told her conversationally.

When she finally dared to turn her head it was to find him gone from the open window. 'Gary,' she called sharply. 'Gary?'

There was no answer. Was he playing a game with her, waiting for her in silence inside her flat? If he thought she was lying about the vertigo, that believing him gone, she would climb back inside, he was wrong. She really couldn't move!

'Gary,' she called again. 'Gary, please answer me.'

He had gone, she was sure of it. God, what could the time be, about three o'clock? That meant she had another three hours before Adam was due to arrive. She wasn't sure she could balance on this ledge for that amount of time. But if she couldn't, that left only one way off it, and that was down!

CHAPTER TEN

IT was amazing how traffic could pass by and not even realise there was a young woman balancing precariously on a second-floor ledge above them! It was a street that had little or no pedestrians, and the people in their cars were too engrossed in their own lives to look up and see Leonie.

One really bad moment came when Harvey decided to make his way back along the ledge, rubbing against her legs in greeting, not understanding when she wouldn't move out of his way and allow him into his home. He became quite agitated by her refusal to move, and with his usual stubbornness refused to go back the way he had come. Leonie vehemently decided that his wandering days were over if she ever got off this ledge.

And so were someone else's if she survived this! Her fury turned to Adam. If they had been living together as husband and wife instead of conducting this ridiculous affair this wouldn't have happened to her. And if an affair were all he wanted he could find some other woman to have it with, she would be his wife or nothing!

What time was it now? She felt as if she had been in this ledge for hours. Surely it must be almost six by now? She was too afraid to even raise her arm and look at her wrist watch! But as if in answer to her question she could hear a clock striking the hour, one, two, three, four, five—she waited for the sixth bell—nothing happened. Five o'clock, it was only five o'clock!

ه wasn't sure she could stay balanced here
r another hour.

Suddenly she heard a noise in the flat behind
her, freezing, almost afraid to breathe. Gary had
been playing a game with her all along, he was
still in there waiting for her.

'What the——! What the hell are you doing out
there?'

She turned sharply at the sound of that voice,
regaining her balance with effort, feeling shaken
as the world swayed up to meet her.

'Be careful, damn it,' Adam rasped. 'You
almost fell then.'

'You don't say,' she scorned shakily. 'You aren't
supposed to be here for another hour,' she accused.

'What?' he frowned his disbelief, in the act of
climbing out of the window.

'It's only five, you said you wouldn't be here
until six,' she stupidly reminded. Had she lost
her mind? What did it matter what the time was,
he was *here*!

'Well if that's the way you feel about being
rescued,' he ground out, climbing back down.
'I'll come back in an hour!'

'Adam!' she screamed her fear that he would
really leave her alone again out here. 'Oh, Adam,'
her voice broke on a sob. 'Don't leave me. Please,
don't leave me!'

'It's all right, Leonie,' he soothed, sounded
closer now. 'I'll be with you in a second, and
we'll go in together.'

'We might fall,' she cried.

'We won't,' he told her calmly.

She felt his fingers on her arm, clasping her
hand now as she clung to him, feeling his
strength flow into her. 'Adam,' she sobbed, still
not turning. 'Oh, Adam!' Sobs wracked her body.

'That bastard!' he grated feelingly. 'He didn tell us he had left you out here.'

'Gary? You mean Gary?' she prompted. 'Did you get him?'

'We got him——'

'How?' she breathed raggedly. 'I had no idea it was him, I even invited him in thinking he could help protect me after the man called again. Oh God, Adam, I've never been so scared in my life!'

'I can imagine,' he cut in harshly. 'And once I have you safely inside you can tell me exactly what happened here this afternoon. But right now I have to get you inside.'

'I can't move,' she shook her head.

'Of course you can,' he soothed.

'No.'

'Leonie, you will move,' he instructed coldly. 'Do you understand me?'

Her bottom lip quivered emotionally. 'There's no need to shout at me.'

'I'll shout at you a lot more than this if you don't soon get yourself moving,' he rasped. 'It's damned windy out here.'

She turned to glare at him. 'Do you think I don't know that?' she snapped furiously. It may have been a warm day but the wind had started to blow about an hour ago, increasing in intensity the last ten minutes or so. 'I've been stuck out here for hours,' she told him angrily. 'I've probably caught pneumonia.'

'You probably deserve to,' Adam said callously. 'No one in their right mind balances on a ledge like this one for hours!'

'That's just the sort of remark I should have expected from you,' Leonie eased along the ledge behind him, glaring at him as she allowed him to catch her under the arms and lift her inside. 'You

on't—Oh!' Her legs gave way as she realised
where she was, Adam catching her deftly before
she fell.

'It's all right now, Leonie,' he soothed,
smoothing her hair as he held her. 'I have you
safe.'

She shuddered as she realised she was at last
off the ledge. 'You deliberately made me so angry
that I didn't know what I was doing,' she accused
between her tears.

'As long as it worked I don't care what I
did,' Adam was trembling. 'I've never been so
scared in my life as when I came in and saw
your open window and realised you were out
there.'

'I tried to use psychology with Gary,' she
remembered with a quiver. 'It didn't work.'

Adam's arms tightened about her. 'He's safely
in police custody now.'

'When? How?' she frowned.

Adam led her over to the sofa, sitting her down
before pouring her a drink, standing over her
while she drank the brandy. He took the empty
glass from her fingers, sitting down beside her to
pull her into his arms. 'Did he hurt you?' he
asked gruffly.

She knew exactly what he was asking. 'No,' she
assured him softly. 'Now tell me how you knew it
was Gary? Is he really in police custody?'

'Yes,' Adam sighed his relief. 'The police
arrested him when he arrived home two hours
ago. I was with them, and when they knocked on
the door he just crumpled. He told them
everything when they took him to the police
station. But he didn't tell us he had left you
perched out on a ledge,' he frowned his anger.

'It's over now, Adam,' she touched his thigh.

'Thank God,' he breathed. 'Having yo
followed told us nothing——'

'You're still looking for the grounds to divorce
me?' she pulled away from him, her expression
pained. 'I hope your detective told you that
you're my only visitor! Can you be named in your
own divorce?' her voice rose shrilly.

'Leonie——'

'I don't think you can, Adam.' She stood up,
moving away from him. 'So we had better stop
our affair so that I can find a lover you *can* name.
Maybe I should have just let Gary do what he
wanted to do after all,' her voice broke. 'Then
you could have named *him*.'

'Leonie——'

'Silly me thought that climbing out on that
ledge was better than being violated,' she said
self-derisively. 'If I had just let him go ahead I
could have saved us all a lot of trouble. You really
should have told me——'

'Leonie, if you say one more word, *one more
word*,' he repeated icily, 'I'll put you over my
knee and beat the living daylights out of you.'

'I wonder why I never realised how gallant
you are.' Her eyes flashed. 'I've just escaped
attack by a sex-maniac by balancing on a ledge
for more than two hours and you intend to beat
me!' She gave a choked laugh. 'And to think
I'd decided, if I ever got off that ledge, that I
was going to talk to you about what went
wrong in our marriage. It looks as if I needn't
bother. Although you'll have to provide the
evidence for the divorce, the thought of taking
a lover nauseates me!'

'Leonie . . .?'

'Although I know it won't be Liz,' she looked
at him accusingly. 'All this time you've let me

believe the two of you were lovers, and you were lying! Liz told me the truth today.'

'If she said we didn't sleep together then *she* lied,' he bit out.

'I know you went to bed together, before we were married. I also know now that it only happened the once. And Liz told me it wasn't done out of love on either of your parts.'

'I still slept with your sister,' Adam told her flatly.

'You helped a friend when she needed it,' Leonie amended abruptly.

'By making love to her!'

'Do you want a whip to beat yourself with?' Leonie scorned. 'What you did wasn't wrong.' She shook her head. 'Misguided, perhaps, but not wrong. I've believed all this time that you were in love with Liz.'

'I never was,' he denied softly.

'I know that now!'

He sighed. 'The night I made love to her should never have happened, I knew that. Never more so than when I met you,' he rasped. 'I think I fell in love with you on sight, and yet my guilt about Liz stood between us.'

Leonie moistened suddenly dry lips. 'You *did* love me?'

'Yes.'

'You never once told me that.'

He frowned. 'Didn't I? But surely it must have been obvious,' he dismissed impatiently.

His emotionally repressed childhood again! 'I ought to hit you over the head with something!' she snapped.

'Why?' he looked dazed.

'Because I loved you from the moment we met too,' she glared at him. 'But my inexperience, my clumsiness, my naiveté, seemed to be driving you away!'

He shook his head. 'Your inexperience enchanted me, your clumsiness amused me, and your naiveté enthralled me!'

'Then why couldn't you bear to be near me!'

'Because of Liz,' he admitted heavily. 'I was terrified that one day you would find out about that night I spent with her, and that you would hate me for it.'

'Why couldn't you have just told me about it before we were married?' she sighed.

'I'd promised Liz. Although, believe me, if I had thought you could accept what happened I would have broken that promise,' he added grimly.

'You thought me too immature to understand,' she nodded. 'I believe I was,' she acknowledged heavily. 'But I understand now.'

His eyes were narrowed. 'You do?'

She gave a ragged sigh. 'Liz told me about Nick, his affair, how you tried to help her through it.'

His mouth twisted. 'I'd like to say it was all a question of helping Liz, but it wasn't. I couldn't have made love to her if I hadn't desired her.'

'I understand that too,' Leonie nodded. 'But you didn't love her, or want to marry her.'

'God, no.'

'I thought you did, you see. That day I saw you together at your office, I thought you had married me because Liz had decided on a reconciliation with Nick rather than marriage to you, that you both now realised your mistake, but that it was too late for you to be together, because Liz was expecting Nick's child. I believed I was a very second, second-best,' she admitted miserably.

'You were never that.' Adam shook his head. 'The night I met you I was driving past Liz's house and saw the lights on. My first thought was that it was burglars. Then you opened the door!' He gave a tight smile. 'I fell, God how I fell. And yet Liz stood between us. I rushed you into marriage before I could talk myself out of it, knew I had to have you even if I lost you later. But our problems began straight away.'

'I was a failure in bed,' she sighed.

'You weren't a failure,' he rasped angrily. 'You were a very young girl with a problem you were too embarrassed to even talk about. And by the time we had dispensed with that problem your barriers were well and truly up, you were self-conscious about lovemaking to the point where you didn't even like me to touch you. You can't know what that did to me! But my own guilt about Liz made it impossible for me to reach you. I knew I was driving you further and further away from me, but I didn't know how to stop it. When you decided to end the marriage I knew I couldn't stop you.'

'And now?'

'Now I'm giving you what you want,' he shrugged. 'An affair.'

'While you divorce me,' she said bitterly.

'For God's sake, I wasn't having you followed so that I can divorce you!' Adam grated. 'I was protecting you, because of those telephone calls.'

'A lot of good that did me,' she scorned, not believing him.

Adam flushed at the rebuke. 'There was a flaw in the plan. On Saturdays I met with the

detective to get his report. We m[e]
thirty today for lunch.'

'So that was who you were mee[.]
realised.

'Yes,' he bit out. 'And while he was te[l.]
that he had followed through investigation[.]
the two men that live here, into the people I [.]
with, and the people you work with, coming
with Gary Kingsfield as the caller, *he* was he[.]
threatening you! No one was here watching you,
damn it,' he admitted tersely.

Leonie could see the humour in the situation
now that she knew Adam wasn't trying to divorce
her. 'That was the flaw?' she couldn't hold back
her smile any longer.

'It isn't funny,' Adam growled. 'He could
have—could have——'

'But he didn't,' she soothed. 'And unless I'm
mistaken, he's done me a favour.'

'I can't think what,' Adam scowled.

She walked into her bedroom without answering, coming back seconds later, opening her hand
in front of him to reveal a thin gold band, and
another ring with the stone of an emerald. 'Will
you marry me?' she invited softly.

His startled gaze was raised to hers. 'The
affair . . .?'

'Is not what I want,' she said with emphasis.
'I only said that in the heat of the moment,
because I was hurt. I'll grant you the last couple
of weeks have been exciting, that first night, the
afternoon at the hotel, the rose every day. But
can't we still have that and be married?'

Adam looked confused. 'I don't understand.'

'Do you still love me?'

'Yes,' came his emphatic answer.

She felt the glow begin inside her. 'And is an

all you want?'

ied. 'I thought after an appropriate
n you'd got used to my being around
me, that I would ask you to be my wife

at's what she had thought, had finally
e to know the workings of her husband's
vious mind. 'I want to be your wife now,' she
old him softly. 'And I want you to be my
husband.'

'Are you sure?'

'As sure as I was when you first asked me to
marry you,' she smiled. 'We've made mistakes,
Adam, terrible, destructive mistakes, but we still
have so much, still love each other so much.
Don't you agree?' she looked at him anxiously.

'Gary Kingsfield will never hurt you again, you
know. He should go to prison for some time once
the police know how he threatened you today.'

'I don't care about Gary,' she dismissed
impatiently. 'I'm talking about us. *Will* you
marry me?'

'Give yourself time to get over the shock of
this afternoon——'

'That does it!' she glared at him, pushing the
two rings on to her finger next to the eternity
ring herself. 'Now we are officially married
again,' she told him crossly. 'And you will be a
good, and always *truthful*, husband,' she
warned.

He raised dark brows. 'I will?'

'You will,' she told him firmly. 'I'll continue to
work, we'll lunch together when we can, you'll
come home to me at five-thirty every evening,
and we'll live together at your apartment. Your
new one, I mean. I don't think we would be
welcome at your father's again,' she grimaced.

'He called this afternoon and invited for dinner next week,' Adam put in softly

Leonie became still. 'Did you accept?'

'I thought I'd ask you first——'

He was learning, this arrogant husband of h

'Then accept,' she instructed. 'I hadn't finish with the outline of our future,' she reprove sternly.

'Sorry,' he said, but there was a devilish glint in his eyes.

'Apology accepted,' she said primly. 'Now I will decorate your apartment as you once suggested I should, and one of those rooms will be a nursery——'

'Children,' he said softly. 'Are we going to have children?'

'Three,' she nodded.

'Why three?' he frowned at the odd number.

'Why not?' she frowned.

Adam shrugged. 'Why not? And when do you plan to have the first of these offspring?'

'Well I thought I needed a bit more practise at the basics first,' she told him thoughtfully.

'Believe me,' he drawled, 'you don't need any more practise.'

She smiled. 'But it might be fun, don't you think?'

'I'm sure it will,' he nodded, taking her into his arms. 'Oh, Leonie, I do love you,' he groaned. 'I'm sorry I was such an idiot when we were together last time.'

'And I'm sorry I was so stupid and left you,' she sighed.

'I'm not,' he shook his head. 'We needed the separation,' he explained at her frown. 'Otherwise we might never have realised how much we love each other.'

She rested her head against his chest as they

...h other silently for a very long time, each
...ing the fact that they had at last managed
...d happiness together.

'...n, Adam,' Leonie greeted him at the door, her
...ce glowing. 'It's triplets!'

The briefcase slipped out of his hand, his face
paling. 'Are you sure?'

'Of course I'm sure,' she said impatiently,
pulling him into the house they had shared with
his father for the last four months, since Leonie
had become pregnant and Charles Faulkner had
humbly asked them to. 'I've seen them.'

Adam swallowed hard. 'You have?'

'Yes,' she laughed exultantly. 'Your father is
delighted.'

'He is?'

'I must say, you seem less than pleased,' she
told him crossly.

He looked dazed. 'I just never thought—One
seemed enough to start with,' he finished lamely.

'One?' she frowned. 'I don't think that's very
usual, they usually come in four or fives.'

Adam frowned. 'Leonie, what are you talking
about?' he sounded puzzled.

'Suki has had her kittens,' she sighed her
impatience with him. 'Harvey is proudly sitting
next to the basket, as if he did it all himself, and
your father gave a cigar to Chambers.' She
giggled as she remembered the look on the
butler's face when Charles Faulkner pushed the
cigar in his breast pocket.

'Dad is excited about his prize Siamese giving
birth to Harvey's kittens?' Adam sounded
disbelieving.

She nodded. 'He says he's going to keep one of
them,' she announced triumphantly. 'Adam,' she

frowned. 'Just what did you think I
about when you came in?'

He looked down at her slightly
stomach. 'Well . . .'

'Adam!' she gave a shocked laugh. 'I've
scan, there's only one in there.'

He took her into his arms. 'One can never
with you,' he nuzzled into her hair. 'That
came as a complete surprise.'

'I think we practised too much,' she mocked.

'What shall we call it now?' he said as he led
her up the stairs to their bedroom.

'Well, we can't allow all that expertise to go
to waste,' she teased as she began to undress
him.

'No,' he agreed as he undressed her.

'So we'll just say we're practising for the next
one,' she murmured as they sank down on the
bed together.

'By the time we're ninety we should be
perfect,' Adam groaned.

Leonie giggled. 'We're perfect now, but so
what . . .'

Everything was perfect, their love for each
other, the fact that Charles Faulkner seemed to
have accepted her as a member of his family since
she was carrying his grandchild.

'By the way,' she caressed his chest. 'I've
booked Mr and Mrs Smith a room at The Savoy
tomorrow afternoon.'

Adam gave a throaty chuckle. 'I think we're
going to have to stop being afternoon lovers
soon.' He looked down at her with tender eyes,
one hand lightly cupping her rounded stomach.
'As it is our baby was conceived in a hotel room.'

'I remember,' she smiled. 'I remember every
minute we spend together.'

꞉,' he told her gruffly. 'So do I—and I ꞉d for all of them! I'm so proud to have my wife, darling.'

his pride and love for her were all that ꞉red.

H·A·R·L·E·Q·U·I·N

FIRST·CLASS
Sweepstakes

OFFICIAL RULES

1. NO PURCHASE NECESSARY. To enter, complete the official entry/order form. Be sure to indicate whether or not you wish to take advantage of our subscription offer.

2. Entry blanks have been preselected for the prizes offered. Your response will be checked to see if you are a winner. In the event that these preselected responses are not claimed, a random drawing will be held from all entries received to award not less than $150,000 in prizes. This is in addition to any free, surprise or mystery gifts which might be offered. Versions of this sweepstakes with different prizes will appear in Preview Service Mailings by Harlequin Books and their affiliates. Winners selected will receive the prize offered in their sweepstakes brochure.

3. This promotion is being conducted under the supervision of Marden-Kane, an independent judging organization. By entering the sweepstakes, each entrant accepts and agrees to be bound by these rules and the decisions of the judges, which shall be final and binding. Odds of winning in the random drawing are dependent upon the total number of entries received. Taxes, if any, are the sole responsibility of the prize winners. Prizes are nontransferable. All entries must be received by August 31, 1986.

4. The following prizes will be awarded:

   (1) Grand Prize: Rolls-Royce™ or $100,000 Cash!
   (Rolls-Royce being offered by permission of Rolls-Royce Motors Inc.)

   (1) Second Prize: A trip for two to Paris for 7 days/6 nights. Trip includes air transportation on the Concorde, hotel accommodations…PLUS…$5,000 spending money!

   (1) Third Prize: A luxurious Mink Coat!

5. This offer is open to residents of the U.S. and Canada, 18 years or older, except employees of Harlequin Books, its affiliates, subsidiaries, Marden-Kane and all other agencies and persons connected with conducting this sweepstakes. All Federal, State and local laws apply. Void in the province of Quebec and wherever prohibited or restricted by law. Winners will be notified by mail and may be required to execute an affidavit of eligibility and release, which must be returned within 14 days after notification. Canadian winners will be required to answer a skill-testing question. Winners consent to the use of their name, photograph and/or likeness for advertising and publicity purposes in conjunction with this and similar promotions without additional compensation. One prize per family or household.

6. For a list of our most current prize winners, send a stamped, self-addressed envelope to: WINNERS LIST, c/o Marden-Kane, P.O. Box 10404, Long Island City, New York 11101

JOCELYN HALEY, known by her fans as **SANDRA FIELD** and **JAN MACLEAN,** now presents her ninth compelling novel.

DREAM of DARKNESS

With the help of the enigmatic Bryce Sanderson,
Kate MacIntyre begins her search for the meaning behind
the nightmare that has haunted her since childhood.
Together they will unlock the past and forge a future.

**Available at your favorite
retail outlet in NOVEMBER.**

You're invited to acce...
4 books and a
surprise gift **Free!**

Acceptance Card

Mail to: Harlequin Reader Service®

In the U.S.
2504 West Southern Ave.
Tempe, AZ 85282

In Canada
P.O. Box 2800, Postal Station A
5170 Yonge Street
Willowdale, Ontario M2N 6J3

YES! Please send me 4 free Harlequin Presents® novels and my free surprise gift. Then send me 8 brand new novels every month as they come off the presses. Bill me at the low price of $1.75 each ($1.95 in Canada)—an 11% saving off the retail price. There are no shipping, handling or other hidden costs. There is no minimum number of books I must purchase. I can always return a shipment and cancel at any time. Even if I never buy another book from Harlequin, the 4 free novels and the surprise gift are mine to keep forever.

108 BPP-BPGE

_____
Name   (PLEASE PRINT)

_____
Address   Apt. No.

_____
City   State/Prov.   Zip/Postal Code

This offer is limited to one order per household and not valid to present subscribers. Price is subject to change.
                                              ACP-SUB-1